W9-DIJ-205

Where the Heart Is

**Center Point
Large Print**

**This Large Print Book carries the
Seal of Approval of N.A.V.H.**

JANE FEATHER
WRITING AS CLAUDIA BISHOP

Where the Heart Is

CENTER POINT PUBLISHING
THORNDIKE, MAINE

This Center Point Large Print edition
is published in the year 2002 by arrangement with
The Berkley Publishing Group, a division of Penguin Putnam Inc.

The text of this Large Print edition is unabridged. In other
aspects, this book may vary from the original edition. Printed in
Thailand. Set in 16-point Times New Roman type by
Bill Coskrey and Gary Socquet.

ISBN 1-58547-230-1

Library of Congress Cataloging-in-Publication Data.

Bishop, Claudia.
    Where the heart is / Jane Feather writing as Claudia Bishop.--Center Point large print ed.
    p. cm.
    ISBN 1-58547-230-1 (lib. bdg. : alk. paper)
    1. Large type books. I. Title.

PS3556.E22 W47 2002
813'.54--dc21

                                                      2002023427

❦ 1 ❦

The gently stroking hand on her back brought Vicki Randall slowly into the land of the living. Reluctantly, she relinquished her dreams as the hand snaked over her body, drawing her ever more closely against the naked figure behind her, then resuming its caressing motions across her belly. She sighed softly as tantalizing fingers began to tease her still somnolent nipples.

"Awake, my love?" Max's breath whispered in her ear.

Vicki curled up into a tight, resistant ball. "I wasn't, but you're doing a good job of waking me," she murmured drowsily. "It may have escaped your notice, Max, but it's Sunday. Normal people sleep late on Sundays, particularly when they get up at six-thirty every other day of the week!"

"It's eight o'clock, Victoria, hardly early." His hand pushed her knees down straight, and his fingers, with a touch as light as thistledown, moved to the inside of her thighs, awakening her response in spite of her halfhearted protests.

"I suppose I should be grateful for a whole hour and a half of extra sleep," she sighed.

"Be quiet and turn over." The words were growled against her cheek, and with a smile she rolled onto her back. Her husband's sleepy face hung over her, his sparkling blue eyes glowing with passion and humor. "If I didn't know what a sexy creature you are, my love, I'd find your performance convincing!"

"You're all scratchy." She laughed, running her hand over his unshaven chin.

"Sorry," Max said in a tone that didn't sound remotely apologetic, "but I'm not shaving until afterward. Did you think you'd married a gentleman?"

"Don't tell me you're asleep again? I thought I'd woken you up!"

Max's teasing voice brought her up onto one elbow. Running a hand through her wavy hair, Vicki gazed up at him with a grin. "You did, but then you exhausted me all over again."

Max Randall laughed, his eyes softening as he looked down at the sleepy, heart-shaped face of his wife. Her slanted green eyes bore their habitual expression of wonder and anticipation as she contemplated the new day. It took her a while to get to that point, though, Max reflected with an inner smile.

"Drink your orange juice, the coffee's on." He handed her a tall glass.

"You're dressed already," Vicki said in disgust, examining his clean-shaven face and the thatch of black hair damp from the shower.

"Well, I wouldn't have said I was dressed, exactly." Max looked down at his body, which was clad only in a pair of brief swimming trunks.

"Oh, you know what I mean! Is that the paper?" She reached for the thick pile of the Sunday *New York Times* lying at her feet.

"If you can unglue your eyes enough, take a look at the Arts and Leisure section." Max tossed the paper onto her stomach before leaving the room.

Vicki battled through the neatly folded sections until she

found the right one, and then sat back comfortably against the leather-padded headboard, hitching the pillows behind her. An old photo of herself, resurrected from the files, no doubt, gazed up from the page. She read the accompanying text with an increasingly clouded expression.

"Honestly, Max!" she exclaimed as he returned, carrying a laden tray. "This is really a bit much. You'd think someone would have asked before writing this."

"Don't be silly, Victoria. If newspapers had to ask everyone they wrote about for permission, there'd never be any gossip. Anyway, the article's not about you, it's about your painting."

"That's drawing a very fine line." Vicki frowned thoughtfully. "Dan had a hand in this. He's drumming up publicity for the Washington show. That man's got dollar signs instead of a heart!"

"Well, neither of you do too badly as a result," Max observed calmly, putting the tray down in the middle of the bed.

Vicki thought of her agent and the manager of the New York gallery where most of her work was exhibited. Max was right, of course. Her job was to paint; Dan's, to sell the result. "Well, he might have warned me," she said in a milder tone.

"It's a very flattering piece." Max took the paper and began to read. "Vicki Carrolton, one of the most exciting of our young, modern painters, is reaching maturity. Her twin themes of humanity's ability to improve the environment while simultaneously destroying it are reaching full expression as she plumbs the depths of the paradox. The swirling, amoebalike configurations of her brush . . ."

"Don't, Max!" Vicki snatched the paper from his hands. "It's a promotion piece, nothing more."

"What an odd creature you are." Max began to pour coffee. "You have a gigantic talent—you know it and so does everyone else—but you can't stand to have it talked about."

Vicki said nothing. It was impossible to make people understand why she was reluctant to have her work discussed. Her attitude didn't make much sense to her, either. Absentmindedly, she stretched out a hand toward the tray, intending to take one of the steaming croissants that lay in enticing buttery warmth on the plate.

"Oh, no, you don't!" Max seized her hand. "You're all black with newsprint. Go wash up."

"You're so prim, Max." Vicki laughed. "I can eat a croissant with dirty hands if I want to."

"No, you can't. Newspapers are full of germs, didn't you know?"

"You're serious?" Vicki said wonderingly.

"Sure I'm serious. Unlike you, I didn't have the benefit of being raised by a trio of older brothers. A strict English nanny taught me my manners!"

"I think I prefer my upbringing—even if it was designed to turn me into the female version of a Carrolton." She swung her legs to the floor. "But since I'm unlikely to get my grubby fingers on a croissant, nanny, I'll go clean up."

"Will I pass?" she asked a few minutes later, emerging from the large, luxurious bathroom adjoining their bedroom. She extended her hands toward Max, controlling her merriment with difficulty. He examined them critically, turning them over, peering at her fingernails, his face grave.

"You still have a black thumbprint on your nose, but apart from that, you'll do." His quick grin drew an instant response from Vicki as she hopped back into bed.

"I don't eat with my nose!" She broke the flaky dough, inhaling deeply of its rich, sweet fragrance as she popped the morsel between eager lips. "*That* is good! What are we going to do today?" The question was accompanied by a slight lift of delicately arched eyebrows as Vicki licked the butter off her fingers before resuming her attack on the croissant.

"Oh, a little skinny-dipping in the pool, a little loving, a little wine, a little cold lobster," Max said lazily, not taking his eyes off the newspaper.

Vicki smiled softly—such a sexy, sensual, seductive man she had married. Leaning forward, she ran a buttery finger along the knobby vertebrae of his spine, insinuating a light, tantalizing fingertip between the elastic of his trunks and the smooth flesh of his hips.

"Careful, you'll spill the coffee," he murmured, still scanning the newsprint.

"Oh, you're *so* romantic," Victoria groaned in mock complaint, enjoying the game, feeling his body tense beneath her fingers.

"If you think it's romantic to have a pot of coffee upturned in the middle of the bed, green eyes, I don't." Max straightened up slowly, methodically tidying the paper and placing the tray at his feet before reaching a seemingly idle hand to pull the cover off her.

Vicki lay still under his desirous gaze, feeling the pleasurable hardening of her nipples as they rose beneath Max's slow appraisal. In the ten freewheeling years during which she had painted her way around Europe, discovering the pleasures of being accountable only to herself, and growing, sometimes painfully, into the mature Vicki Carrolton, she had never met anyone like Max Randall. Never had she loved as she did now, or felt so loved.

"You have the most wonderful, wanting body, Victoria, and the most loving spirit." The tenderness in Max's voice had her moving down the bed, offering herself to his warm and loving touch. "I don't believe this is mine." His hands ran slowly over her compliant flesh as she lay quiet, enjoying her passivity, allowing him to push apart her thighs, to find and caress the moist center of her desire. His face was full of wonder as he ran his dampened hand over her stomach, circling her navel with a light finger. Then, reverently, he cupped the swelling mounds of her breasts.

"Such beautiful little breasts," Max whispered, bending his head to take their erect peaks into his mouth, his tongue darting in a series of swift, flicking strokes. Vicki moved beneath him, her hands slipping inside his swimming trunks, finding and caressing the hard evidence of his arousal. Max groaned softly as she cupped him in her palms, her fingers squeezing lightly but demandingly.

"Sit up." He accompanied the soft instruction with a firm lift of her body, tightly gripping her around her ribcage. She moved her hands slowly up his body, curling her fingers in the thick mat of chest hair, teasing his nipples, throwing back her head so his firm lips and flicking tongue could possess the soft, vulnerable area under her chin.

"I wish you'd take those trunks off," Vicki murmured, trying to push them off his hips—a difficult task since he was still sitting on the edge of the bed. Obligingly, Max got to his feet, allowing her to rid them both of the obstruction. Trembling now with excitement and anticipation, Vicki knelt on the bed, taking him between firm lips, grasping his buttocks with hard, demanding fingers. It was Max's turn to give himself up to her caress, and he did so with a shuddering sigh of pleasure.

"Oh, you're so beautiful, my love," she whispered breathlessly, raising her head to look deeply into those intense, blue eyes.

"That makes two of us." Max smiled softly as he lifted her easily under the arms and sat back on the edge of the bed, maneuvering her astride his lap.

"Playtime?" Vicki laughed softly.

"A little conspicuous athleticism, I think," he answered, holding her hips firmly, moving her against him until she had established her own rhythm. This was a laughing loving as they struggled to maintain the awkward position until suddenly Vicki gripped his shoulders.

"Darling." It was both question and statement, and he smiled softly in response, his eyes becoming almost purple as they met hers in confirmation. And then there was nothing either of them could have done to prevent the convulsive fusion of their finale.

"Oh, Max, my love." Vicki sighed, shaking her head with the awe and amazement that her husband always inspired in her. "I wonder if you'll always be able to do that to me?"

"Always," he affirmed quietly, kissing her tenderly as he drew both of them to their feet. "Go take a shower now. I'll clear away the tray and we can begin the rest of the day."

"Yes, nanny." With a laugh, she sprang out of his reach and headed for the bathroom. The steaming-hot water seemed to reach the marrow of her satisfied bones as she twisted and turned under the massaging spray. Resolutely, she rotated the hot-water knob to the left and the cold-water knob to the right, enduring a few seconds of icy water that pummeled her back to reality before stepping out with relief. She toweled herself briskly, enjoying the roughness of her movements that left her skin glowing pink.

It was amazing how easily one could get used to luxury again, Vicki mused, slipping into a soft silk kimono as she glanced around the large bedroom. The main part of the room was furnished much like a sitting room, couches and chairs grouped on subtle-toned Oriental rugs scattered over the deeply waxed oak floors. A thickly carpeted sleeping platform reached by three shallow steps ran the length of one wall. Their bed was a custom-made, seven-foot-wide, firmly sprung mattress resting on a low base, its headboard the same width of wall, well padded with squabs of bronze leather. July sunlight poured in through the long window on the south wall.

Vicki turned the antique porcelain knob on the heavy door as she left the room to make her way along the gallery and down the shallow, curved staircase to the first floor. They had spent much time and considerable expense renovating the house in such a way that its essential character was undisturbed. The kitchen was the only room that bore no resemblance to its nineteenth-century equivalent. The door leading to the kitchen from the hallway was the original, but once beyond that door one was beamed into the twentieth century with a vengeance.

Vicki stood, feeling the cork tiles warm on her bare feet as she watched Max. He was back in his trunks, calmly loading the dishwasher, emptying coffee grounds into the disposal, and rinsing out the coffee pot. The surfaces gleamed with space-age efficiency; the sliding glass doors to the patio stood open onto the large oval swimming pool. Vicki crossed the room, sliding her arms around her husband's narrow waist.

"Leave the dishes, househusband," she murmured mischievously in his ear. "There are better things to do with a Sunday morning."

"One of these days, Victoria . . . !" Max turned under the pressure of her hands, eyes dancing as he gripped her shoulders, shaking his head in mock exasperation. "Come on, let's swim."

Laughing, they went out to the patio. Vicki stripped off her robe, cleaved the water with a neat racing dive, then floated lazily on her back as she squinted up into the deep blue summer sky.

The house stood on two acres of wooded garden, ensuring total privacy, which, she reflected with a secret grin, was all to the good—considering their somewhat uninhibited lifestyle. Their housekeeper lived in a comfortable apartment over the old stables that had been converted to a garage, and, when not on duty, kept very much to herself.

"Swim, you lazy creature! You'll get fat if you don't get some exercise." Max surfaced beside her, sporting a broad grin as he placed a firm palm on her stomach, pushing her under the water.

"Brute!" She came up gasping. "I'll race you, three laps." Her powerful overarm was no match for Max's seemingly effortless crawl, however, and she collapsed gasping on a lounge, reveling in the hot sun as it dried her naked, glistening back.

Max stood dripping above her, gazing at the golden tan that covered every inch of her skin. "You haven't conveniently forgotten that we have to go to that dinner party tonight, I suppose?"

Vicki rolled onto her back, peering up at him. He was smiling, but there was a hint of seriousness in those blue eyes and a firm set to the long jaw. He looked almost as if he were anticipating trouble. "No, I haven't forgotten." She sighed. "Don't look so stern, Max. I told you I was prepared to play 'corporate wife' when necessary. I just don't want to make that role my whole life."

He nodded. "I just wanted to be sure I wasn't in for any surprises."

Victoria watched him through narrowed eyes as he stretched out on the lounge beside her. It wasn't her idea of a fun evening—a business dinner hosted by one of Max's associates—but she had bought the whole package when she had married Max Randall, head of the vast Randall family empire, and she had bought it with her eyes open. The only daughter and fourth child of an old New England family, she had early rebelled against the social obligations and conventions that were inextricable partners of wealth. For ten years, she had shelved the affluence in exchange for her freedom. If anyone had told the young Vicki Carrolton that she would end up married to one of the wealthiest men on the East Coast, accepting the duties and restraints of that role, though with reluctance, she would have laughed at the absurd prediction.

"I suppose you're going to insist we spend the night in the city?" she asked resignedly.

Max put down his book. "Be sensible, darling. I have to be in the office by nine o'clock tomorrow. It makes no sense to drive thirty miles to Croton at midnight and then thirty miles back to Manhattan in the morning, does it?"

"I guess not. How do I get back tomorrow, then?"

"We'll use your car this evening. I'll park it under the office and you can pick it up any time you like. Ed can drive me home tomorrow night."

Vicki nodded her acquiescence. As usual, Max was being utterly logical and reasonable. Besides, she had to be in the city tomorrow herself. Yet her spirit mutinied even as her mind capitulated to reason. Perhaps Vicki Carrolton, bohemian rebel, had not changed so much with the years after all.

❧ 2 ❧

"What are you wearing?" Max asked that evening as he turned from the mirror and carefully inserted silver studs in his white dress shirt.

"Don't know. You want to choose?" Vicki slowly slid the sheer pantyhose over one foot, balancing easily on her other leg. Max was considerably more interested in her clothes than she was—Vicki shopped reluctantly and only when absolutely necessary. Her husband, on the other hand, took infinite pleasure in buying her clothes. His taste was impeccable, and early on in their relationship Vicki had ceased to object, realizing just how much he enjoyed the activity. Now, he opened her closet door, running a swift, appraising eye over its contents.

"Come here and let me look at you."

"Why do you want to look at me?" she questioned with a grin, knowing the answer.

"I want to see what color you are tonight," he replied solemnly, and her grin widened. Max took everything so seriously; what dress she wore tonight would depend entirely on the tones of her complexion, whether she was glowing with vibrant health, or slightly drawn with the fatigue of overwork, or tinged with the gray cast of pre-menstrual tension.

Max cupped her face, examining her closely. "Are you laughing at me, Victoria?"

She sparkled up into his dancing eyes. "Sure I am. You're quite funny, you know."

"Obsessive-compulsive, you mean!" A light finger teased her eyelids; blue eyes glinted with self-mockery.

"But you're very lovable in spite of it."

"Thank you, ma'am." He inclined his head slightly and pulled a mass of gauzy chiffon from the closet. "This, I think." He dropped the dress over her head, tied the ribbon shoulder straps, pulled up the long zipper, and stood back, appraising his handiwork.

"Satisfied?" Vicki inquired with a small, questioning shrug.

"Take a look." Strong hands turned her toward the mirror.

His choice was, as always, perfect. The vivid rainbow colors accentuated the peachy-gold tan of her bare shoulders, the deep green of her eyes, and the strawberry blond of the wavy tresses flowing from her neat, well-shaped head. The elasticized bodice molded small, taut breasts and drew attention to her tiny waist. Soft folds of material swung from hip to mid-calf.

"So, puppet master, what next?" Victoria stood before him, arms hanging down her body like a marionette's, drooping head hiding the laughter in her eyes.

Max chuckled softly. "Put some shadow on your eyes and wear the emerald pendant; after that, you're on your own."

The car purred down the narrow, pretty country lanes, through the village of Croton-on-Hudson. This part of affluent Westchester County was an enchanting, countrified haven bordering the wide sweep of the Hudson River and dominated by the magnificent Palisades. Vicki sat back in the passenger seat, eyes closed, stilling her mind and body to a state of half-sleep that, on many occasions, enabled her to do with the barest minimum of real sleep—at times the creative pressures of her work would not allow her the conventional eight hours of oblivion.

They drew to a smooth halt in front of the imposing apartment building on Fifth Avenue, facing Central Park. Max leaned over her, opening the passenger door. "Go on up and make our excuses. We're already late. I'll park the car under the office and grab a cab back. It won't take long."

Vicki shrugged acceptingly and got out of the car. They were so different from each other, she reflected, making her way into the building, and identifying herself to the doorman. Max was tidy, orderly, detested unpunctuality; she had never been able to understand what difference a few minutes could make, and, while she liked a degree of surface tidiness, believed firmly in the principle that what the eye can't see, the heart won't grieve over. Her closets and drawers bore ample witness to this maxim. The only area where it didn't apply was in her studio—there the most critical observer would find only the most workmanlike order.

The door to the Adamses' apartment swung open as the elevator released her. Clearly, an alerting message had been sent from downstairs.

"Mrs. Randall, I'm Laura Adams." An elegant, well-coiffed, fashionably slim woman came, hand outstretched, toward her. Vicki took the proffered hand, murmuring a courteous response as she explained why she was alone. She allowed herself to be drawn into the large, thronged living room with its enormous picture window overlooking Central Park. As she did so, her eye caught a broad canvas occupying a prominent, well-lighted position on the far wall. Her slight hesitation didn't pass unnoticed by her companion.

"Ah, yes, one of yours, Vicki—you don't mind if I call you Vicki?"

Vicki shook her head. "Of course not. Everyone does except Max, who calls me Victoria. May I?" She moved toward the painting, her hostess following close behind.

"You were a lot less expensive in those days." Laura Adams laughed lightly as they stood in front of the painting.

"Rightly so," Vicki replied truthfully. It was a very youthful "Vicki Carrolton," painted before she had per-fected the technique with color that had pushed her with such meteoric force into the forefront of the up-and-coming painters of her generation. She remembered the painting well; she had just started studying with David Marshall—that giant among contemporary artists—and was still trying to sort out the confusing turmoil created by her refusal to follow the established patterns of a Carrolton woman. Shaking off the memories, she turned quickly to her hostess.

"It's always a little strange to see one's work in a different setting, particularly after such a long time; but it's very flattering." Smiling with the warmth that never failed to endear her to her companions, she indicated her willingness to join the party.

Her dual role as the wife of Max Randall and as Vicki Carrolton, the painter, created its customary effect as she was presented—like some prize specimen, Vicki decided—to the interested groups in the room. Just as she was beginning to think the smile on her face would become a permanent fixture, firm pressure was applied to the back of the slim column of her neck.

"Come and meet the Sandersons," Max said softly, slipping a possessive arm around her waist, drawing her, with a polite excuse to the people around her, across the room. "I'm in the process of some very tricky negotiations with Doug Sanderson, and I need your charm to sugar the pill."

"Surprise, surprise," she muttered. "I hadn't assumed we were here for the fun of it."

"Back up, Victoria." The pressure of his hand on her waist increased, sending warmth through the thin material to the bare skin beneath.

"Just kidding, darling," she whispered.

Max had no time to respond as they reached the group by the window, and for the next half-hour, Vicki concentrated on soothing the obviously ruffled feathers of Doug Sanderson. She flattered, cajoled, and gently flirted until, all smiles, he was taking her in to dinner.

Max took his place opposite her, exerting his own brand of irresistible charm on Mrs. Sanderson. For an instant, Vicki's eyes met Max's in brief acceptance of the duties necessitated by this business evening. Vicki smiled to herself, suppressing the familiar surge of desire aroused by his look. None of his features seemed to have been designed to go with any other. The strong, assertive profile was dominated by a nose that just missed being aquiline; a pair of deepset blue eyes that on occasion turned almost purple pierced the world from beneath a broad, jutting forehead and bushy black eyebrows. A long, unconciliatory jaw and a wide, generous mouth opening over even white teeth completed the picture of the most exciting man Vicki had ever met, the man who had so coolly, logically, and relentlessly overcome her determination to remain single and unfettered by the bonds and duties of marriage. But then, women went down like ninepins before this quiet, assertive man whose air of self-possessed authority was so thoroughly ingrained after twelve years as head of the mighty Randall Corporation—why should she have been any different?

Vicki gave a quick mental shrug and turned her attention to her neighbor. Her role tonight was very clear—she was expected to soften up Doug Sanderson and to behave as the charming, sophisticated wife of a successful husband. It was a role she had been educated to play, and had watched her mother play to perfection. In her salad days, Vicki had firmly resolved never to take that part herself—but she didn't know Max Randall then!

Helping herself sparingly from the dishes presented by the smiling, attentive maid, she employed all the social skills acquired in her youth as she refrained from a barbed comment when Doug's knee brushed against hers once too often for accident, responded lightly to the heavy innuendoes that seemed to make up the greater part of his conversation, and removed her hand with the utmost discretion from his clammy hold.

By the end of dinner, the strain was beginning to tell. Vicki rose, with an alacrity that brought a gleam of understanding humor to her husband's eyes, when their hostess suggested they return to the living room.

"Who's the collector in your family, Laura?" They were sitting amid coffee cups and liqueur glasses when Vicki turned the small talk into an avenue that might provide some interest.

"Oh, that's John. He's been collecting for years," Laura replied enthusiastically. "What do you think of them? You're the expert, after all."

Victoria shook her head in quiet disclaimer. "I'm a painter, not an art critic, Laura. It doesn't give me the expertise to comment on other people's taste. But I will say that on the whole I share your husband's."

Max turned slightly from the group by the window, watching her. She appeared quite relaxed, he thought, but he could tell by the slight stiffness of her shoulders that she was reaching her limit—not that she would ever let on to her companions. He frowned unconsciously. For some reason, he always felt guilty subjecting her to an evening of this kind—she was very open with him about her dislike of these occasions, but never resentful or awkward. Perhaps that was why he felt guilty, Max decided, and went over to the sofa where his wife was sitting, rescue in mind.

"I was about to tell Vicki that we'd quite given up on you, Max, until she came along," Laura said brightly. "You were the most eligible bachelor in New York and persistently refused to take all the lures thrown to you. Why, you were the despair of every unmarried woman in town! Everyone wants to know Vicki's secret."

Max shot a quick warning look at his wife, seeing the angry flash in those cat's eyes. He laid a hand on her head. To an observer, it would seem a casual, tender gesture; but Victoria was aware Max was demanding her silence. "I can assure you, Laura," he said quickly, with a light, easy laugh, "the only person throwing out lures was me. Persuading Victoria to merge her interests with mine was certainly the toughest deal I've ever had to negotiate!" He felt her body relax under his hand and gave a silent sigh of relief. He well understood her annoyance, but he had no desire to hear her express it in that soft, well-modulated voice that could, on occasion, be quite devastating.

"Come talk to John, Victoria." He pulled her to her feet, with a smile of excuse to Laura. "He wants your opinion on a painting he's just acquired—by your friend Tyson, I think."

Vicki readily allowed herself to be removed from the danger zone, and willingly examined the small, color-washed seascape. While she didn't much like being asked for her opinion, talking about art was certainly safer than sitting beside Laura Adams! "It's a good Tyson," she said thoughtfully, cocking her small head on one side. "He's at his best working with those muted grays and blues. I like it."

"It's good to get the endorsement of an expert," John said jovially.

"Judging by your collection, John, I would have said *you* were the expert." Vicki handed out the compliment without conscious thought. At this point, she was operating on automatic pilot, knowing through instinct and experience what responses were appropriate and polite. It was no longer necessary to exert herself; her earlier efforts with Doug Sanderson had clearly achieved the desired results, judging by his continuing smile and booming laugh and Max's general air of relaxation.

"Duty done, my love. Come make your farewells." The low voice in her ear accompanied the firm pressure around her waist, and she turned swiftly toward him. "For heaven's sake, don't look so relieved," Max whispered urgently. "I'll have you out of here in five minutes; just keep up the pretense for a little while longer."

Vicki flashed him an enormous smile, glittering with artificiality, and raised her eyebrows questioningly.

"No," he said on a choke of laughter, "that won't do either! *Please* behave!" He steered her across the room, toward their hostess, both of them controlling their laughter. Vicki deliberately gushed her thanks and good-byes, not so much as to be obvious to their hostess but quite enough for Max, whose fingers tightened warningly on her shoulder where his arm rested with casual possession.

"Victoria, you're going to be the death of me!" Max exclaimed as the elevator doors closed behind them.

Vicki grinned at him. "Come on, you know perfectly well that my social manners are as impeccable as my family background. You'd never have married me, otherwise—the most eligible bachelor in New York, after all! How *did* you manage to resist all those lures thrown out to you by those battalions of gorgeous, greedy ladies?"

The elevator doors opened, and for answer Max seized

her elbow in an ungentle hold, marching her across the lobby and out into the muggy night air. "Now," he said, walking briskly along the sidewalk, still gripping her elbow, forcing her to keep pace with him, "just what the hell did you mean, I wouldn't have married you otherwise?"

Vicki glanced up at the unyielding profile, realizing suddenly that he hadn't taken her remark as the joke it was intended to be. His pace forced her to take a few quick, skipping steps to keep up. "It was supposed to be funny," she said eventually, hearing how lame it sounded.

"Then there are clearly times when we don't share the same sense of humor. Of all the absurd, insulting things to say!" He lengthened his stride. Vicki attempted to shake off his hold, pulling backward as irritation rose within her, but his grip tightened as he jerked her forward.

"Max, you're hurting me!" she protested furiously.

"I am *not* hurting you, and I'm *not* going too fast. You forget I've seen you match those brothers of yours during a twelve-mile hike on the Appalachian Trail! I know exactly what you're capable of!"

Vicki sighed. "I'm not wearing hiking boots right now. I could manage better if you'd just let me take these ridiculous sandals off."

Max stopped abruptly, releasing her elbow. Vicki looked up at him, meeting his gaze as she fought down her own annoyance, sensing that somehow her teasing remark had hit a sensitive spot.

"Look," she said with quiet forcefulness, "I don't know what button I pressed, but it wasn't intentional. I'm willing to apologize for whatever it was you thought I was implying."

"Let's talk about this inside; we've only got another half-block to walk." Max took her hand and they resumed their journey, in silence but at a civilized pace at least, toward the building that housed their Manhattan apartment. Previously Max's main home, it now served as a convenient *pied à terre* for evenings like this. Vicki disliked living in the city, and they had bought the Croton farmhouse nine months ago, just before their marriage. She had, however, imprinted her own distinctive style on the apartment during the preceding year, when she had almost, but not quite, moved in with Max during those months when he had mounted his attack on her fierce independence.

The aggressively modern living room sprang to life as Max flicked light switches. Leather, teak, glass, and chrome, a stark black and white color scheme mellowed with touches of ivory and antique gold—it was a room that reflected their shared tastes.

"Pour me an Armagnac, will you? I'm just going to check the telex." Max disappeared in the direction of his small, functional office. Vicki took two heavy crystal goblets from the elegant Danish glass-fronted cabinet and rummaged in the bottom cupboard for the opaque bottle. It looked as if it was going to be a long night, she reflected wearily, pouring the golden liquid up to the first diamond cuts in the goblets.

Taking one glass, she walked over to the window and gazed absently over the brilliantly lighted city, still seething with life as if it were midday. Behind her, soft footsteps crossed the thick pile of the wool carpet. An arm came around her shoulders, drawing her tightly against the strong, muscular frame.

"I'm sorry, love." A hand stroked gently, tenderly, over

her face, and fingers ran placatingly through her hair. Her body became infused with a sense of peace and relief as she turned slowly against Max's chest, lifting her face for the soft, caressing kiss he placed on her eyelids.

"Oh, Max, I'm sorry, too—I don't know how or why that happened."

"I'm not used to you yet." Max sipped his drink, his eyes fixed on the view outside the window. "You have such a quick tongue and such a sharp wit—it throws me some-times. When you're not used to being teased, Victoria, it can be a bit of a shock."

"I suppose I'm learning that." She leaned against him, slipping her free arm around his waist. "It's such a natural thing for me—Carroltons tease each other all the time."

"They also fight a great deal, as I remember," Max remarked dryly.

"Randalls don't fight?" Vicki said incredulously.

"They do, but with more venom than your family. We don't storm and shout—we give each other the deep-freeze treatment and stay angry indefinitely."

Vicki shuddered involuntarily. "Not you, Max, surely?"

"I avoid anger," he replied flatly, "although I admit I came close to it tonight."

"But you're not angry now?" Vicki examined the strong, determined face anxiously, recognizing the residue of hurt in the blue eyes.

"No. I jumped too quickly. You touched a sore spot, but I understand you didn't mean to." He took her empty glass, placing it with his on the long teak coffee table. "Come along, golden girl, it's bedtime."

"You know, I still want to know how you resisted all those

26

gorgeous, greedy ladies," Vicki said consideringly, her eyes on the escape route to the bedroom behind her.

"Don't you move, Victoria, not one inch!" Max's eyes sparked laughter as he strode across the room.

It was indeed going to be a long night, she thought, all weariness forgotten as she leaped for the hallway. Vicki was fast, but Max was faster; his foot was in the bedroom door before she could shut it, his hands catching her wrists, clipping them behind her back as he pressed her close to his firm, unyielding body.

"Now, wife," Max said softly, "run that by me again, if you dare!"

She couldn't move, imprisoned as she was by the hard wall of his body, her wrists pushed into the small of her back, his hands holding her against him. But she had been well taught by her brothers—with a swift movement, her left leg swung out, curling behind his knees, throwing him off balance.

They fell together, laughing, to the floor. "You certainly play rough, green eyes," Max gasped, hitching himself onto one elbow, leaning over her as she lay spread-eagled beneath him.

"I was taught to move fast in a clinch!"

"How could I ever have forgotten that?" he murmured in mock wonder. "Now, why don't you show me just how fast you can get onto that bed?"

The strong, heady aroma of fresh coffee assailed Vicki's nostrils, bringing her out of the light doze that, at the insistent shriek of the alarm clock, had replaced the night's heavy sleep. The room was filled with sunlight; the muted voice of a radio announcer reading the news greeted her as she struggled onto one elbow.

"Good morning, little love." Max came over to the bed, smiling down at her with that special remembering smile. His white terry-cloth bathrobe was only loosely tied, revealing a thick mat of black chest hair, and his head was damp from the shower, the unruly, disheveled thatch giving him an unusually disorganized look that she loved to see.

"What's the time?" Vicki mumbled.

"Eight o'clock." He laughed. "A whole hour and a half later than usual."

"Aren't we the lucky ones? One of the innumerable benefits of staying in the city overnight, I suppose." Her voice was heavy with mock sarcasm.

"Don't be cranky, Victoria." Bending over her, Max kissed her firmly into good humor. "Better now?" His teeth flashed in an affectionate grin as he slowly straightened up.

"Just complete the cure with a cup of coffee," Vicki requested, struggling into a sitting position against the padded headboard, regarding her husband with loving, amused eyes. His cheerful patience never failed to amaze her. There were times when she couldn't put up with herself and wouldn't have really blamed Max for an irritable response, but it rarely came.

"Thanks, love." She smiled softly at him, taking the large French-style bowl filled to the brim with creamy coffee.

Max ruffled her tousled curls with a careless hand before returning to the bathroom.

"Oh, Max?" Vicki called suddenly over the buzz of the

electric razor.

"Mmm?" He came to the open bathroom door, running the small machine over his chin.

"Can you do me a favor this morning?"

"Depends on what it is." He flicked off the razor, raising his eyebrows inquiringly.

"Could you reserve me a table at Dominique's for lunch?"

"Sure. When for?"

"Today, of course."

"*Today,* Victoria? You know you have to reserve a week in advance there. Why on earth are you asking me at the last minute?" The usually calm voice carried a hint of exasperation.

"I'm asking you at the last minute just because it *is* the last minute," Vicki replied reasonably; it seemed perfectly logical to her. "If I'd remembered earlier, I could have done it myself. Come on, Max. You have much more clout than I do. I don't know what sort of a retainer you pay the maître d', but I'm sure it's fairly substantial."

A slight smile tugged at the corners of his wide mouth. "It is, actually, but whether it's substantial enough to pull this one off, I don't know." He sighed. "Okay, I'll do what I can, but I'm not promising anything. What time?"

"One o'clock, table for two," she responded promptly, knowing that if Max said he would try, he would succeed.

Max nodded briefly. "If there's a problem, I'll get Lois to call you." He began to get dressed while Vicki watched him over the rim of the delicate blue and white china bowl. It was one of her favorite moments of the day, lying in bed watching her husband's deft, economical movements as he transformed himself from the uninhibited lover of the night into the president of the Randall Corporation.

"By the way, green eyes," Max came across the room, tucking the crisp, white shirt into the waist of his dark-gray pants, "who are you taking out for an intimate lunch?"

"Ah," Vicki grinned, "that's for me to know and for you to find out."

Max looked at her, a smile playing on his lips. "I don't imagine that should prove too difficult," he murmured, swooping down suddenly, pulling the covers back. Sensing what he was about to do, Vicki squealed, scooting across the wide bed as she futilely tried to escape the swift hands. Max caught her easily and began to tickle her until she was gasping for breath, her body convulsed beneath those merciless fingers.

"Stop, please stop! I'll tell you. I'll tell you!"

Laughing cheerfully, Max released her. "Well?"

Vicki gathered the covers around her again, an expression of comical dignity on her face that brought a shout of laughter from Max. "Come on. I'm waiting!"

"More coffee, please." She held out her empty bowl; Max took it and filled it from the coffee pot standing on a small table by the window.

"Bonnie Danville." Vicki took a deep gulp of the hot, revivifying liquid. Seeing his puzzled look, she continued, "I told you about her, I think. We were at school together. Bonnie and I have known each other since we were about ten. She's an art historian—we shared an apartment in Paris."

Max nodded. "I remember now. She was in Paris when we were married and couldn't get back."

"Right," Vicki said. "Anyway, she called me from Europe

last week to say she'd be in New York for a few months to do some research. We made this date, only I forgot to reserve a table." She shrugged lightly. "It could happen to anyone."

Max shook his head. "It could certainly happen to *you,* but I suppose it's understandable. You've been working a blue streak recently. How's it going?"

Victoria frowned deeply. "I'm going to have to leave it for a few days. I can't get the blessed thing right, Max!"

He sat down on the bed, taking her square, competent hands in his. They were workman's hands, he thought, running a forefinger over the short, neatly filed fingernails; the only visible part of her that indicated the tough, wiry strength in that seemingly delicate body. She had been variously described as ethereal, delicate, and fragile, but she was actually none of these things, as her hands proved. Raising them to his lips, he kissed the soft cushions below her fingers.

"It's a monumental subject, Victoria."

She nodded readily. "To tell the truth, love, I'm not sure I'm experienced enough to deal with it. There's something a little overconfident, don't you think, about a thirty-year-old trying to depict the nuclear holocaust in a series of three paintings?"

"That rather depends on the thirty-year-old." He smiled. "This one will get it right, eventually. You've been working on it for a long time, don't forget."

"I know." Victoria laughed suddenly, throwing off the attack of gloom. "And if this isn't the time to finish it, I'll leave it until I'm ready. Dan's not going to be too happy about that, though," she added thoughtfully.

"That's Dan's problem," Max said briskly. "I must run, darling." He rose quickly, then completed his dressing with swift, methodical movements. As he bent to kiss her good-bye, Vicki inhaled the clean, lemony fragrance of his skin, running her fingers in a gentle caress over his face, lingering on his lips.

"I love you," she whispered.

"And I love you, my lynx-eyed wife," he responded gently.

"I can't understand why." Victoria shook her head slightly. "I'm not exactly the easiest person to live with."

"That's certainly true." Max stood up, a gleam in his piercing blue eyes. "But you're certainly the most exciting!" A quick, affectionate tug on her curls, and he was gone.

Lying relaxed against the pillows, Vicki finished her coffee. But the bright day beckoned and, flinging off the covers, she made for the bathroom. She had told herself that she would not work for the next three days—it was a form of self-discipline that she had forced herself to learn over the years. If something was blocking the flow of ideas onto canvas, it was futile to push things. With her mind clear, whatever was causing the difficulty would surface and could be dealt with. She changed the radio station from Max's discreet news program to a middle-of-the-road pop station suiting her present mood and, singing softly, drew a bath, shaking drops of bath oil into the water.

Steaming midmorning heat struck her when, an hour later, the doors swung shut behind her on the comfortable, con-trolled temperature in the apartment building. Her white cotton sailor shirt with its navy-blue tie and her pleated navy-blue cotton skirt combined cool practicality with elegance, and Vicki swung with her easy stride toward Madison Avenue, her plaited-leather shoulder bag hanging casually from one shoulder. It was a fairly short walk to the gallery, but the muggy air forced her to adapt her pace to the climate. She paused frequently to window shop—an activity she enjoyed considerably more than shopping itself—and eventually reached the building that housed Astral Galleries. Inside, it was cool again, and she paused to dab the beads of perspiration from her upper lip and forehead before climbing the stairs to the second floor.

The large, corridorlike room was empty, not surprising during the dog days of a Manhattan summer, and Vicki moved through to Dan's office at the back.

"Vicki!" She was seized in an enormous bear hug. "When am I going to see the holocaust series?" Daniel Kesselbaum stood away from her, regarding her with the anxious frown that was his habitual expression.

"You'll have to come to the house, Dan. I'm stuck at the moment."

"But, Vicki, I *must* have it for the D.C. show."

"You'll have it when it's ready, Dan." She laughed affectionately at the impossibly tall, thin man towering above her. "You know quite well that nothing leaves my studio until I'm satisfied with it."

"Don't tell me you two are fighting again." Dan's assistant came out of the inner office, a broad grin splitting her cheerful face, teeth gleaming brilliantly against the smooth café-au-lait complexion.

"Hi, Bev." Vicki embraced her warmly. "No, we're not fighting. Dan's pushing me for the last of the holocaust series, but it's not going smoothly."

Dan shrugged, going over to the enormous coffee pot. He seemed to live on caffeine and nicotine, Vicki thought, watching as he poured the strong black liquid into three mugs. She had known Dan for ten years—ten years of an intensely close, frequently tempestuous working relationship and a deep, abiding friendship.

"Okay, Vicki." Dan hitched himself onto the corner of his cluttered desk. He lit a cigarette, then dragged the smoke deeply into his lungs. "Is there any chance they'll be ready for the show? It's not for two and a half months."

Vicki shook her head helplessly. "I really don't know, Dan. I've finished the first two, but the third could take forever. And you're not having the first two without the third," she said swiftly, anticipating his next question. "Tell you what, why don't you and Bev come over for lunch on Sunday? You can take a look then."

"I don't seem to have much choice." He smiled resignedly, the tension leaving his body. "While you're here, I want you to sign some contracts."

It was almost one o'clock when Victoria left the gallery. Casting a swift, practiced eye down the street, she moved between two parked cars and hailed a cruising cab. She gave the address of Dominique's and sank with relief into the relatively cool interior.

The restaurant was humming with low-voiced conversations. Silent, efficient waiters moved briskly but discreetly among the tables.

"Ah, Mrs. Randall, good afternoon. Your guest has just arrived." The maître d', wreathed in smiles, came swiftly toward her before she'd had time to announce herself. She had dined here often enough with Max not to be surprised that the maître d' recognized her, but the old habits of anonymity died hard and she was slightly taken aback. However, with an accepting smile, Vicki followed him through the room to a well-placed, secluded table by the window. Bonnie Danville rose instantly as she saw her, and the two women hugged briefly, saving their enthusiasm until Vicki's black-coated escort had seated her and left.

"So, Vicki?" Bonnie stretched her hand across the white linen and heavy silverware; their fingers met in a tight squeeze.

"So, Bonnie?" Vicki smiled at the deeply tanned face of her oldest and dearest friend. "How are things?"

"Good," Bonnie replied promptly. "But before I tell *you* anything, you have to tell me how the most confirmed bachelor girl of my acquaintance got herself hooked. No one in Paris could believe it—Jean-Pierre was struck dumb for a week!"

Vicki gave a snort of laughter. "That's absurd, Bonnie! Jean-Pierre has never been silent for more than two minutes in his life." She turned with surprise as a waiter appeared, setting down a small table holding an ice bucket and bottle at her side.

"With Mr. Randall's compliments, ma'am," he said, lifting the bottle of Dom Pérignon out of the bucket for her inspection.

Victoria's lips twitched slightly, but she said nothing, just nodded her approval with a polite smile of thanks.

When he'd slipped discreetly away, Bonnie's eyes met hers, brimming with amusement. "Did I just hear what I thought I did?" she inquired.

"You did." Vicki chuckled. "I'm amazed Max hasn't ordered for us, too." She opened the glossy menu, her eyes widening. "Guess what? My husband is paying for our lunch."

"Did he say so?" Bonnie looked up, startled.

"He's not that straightforward." Vicki grinned and shrugged. "I just have one of those menus with no prices listed. How about you?"

Bonnie nodded, eyebrows raised.

"Oh, well, we'll just have to sit back and enjoy it—I can hardly make a scene." Vicki shook her head in mock disbelief. "Are you beginning to get the picture, Bonnie? Max has a way of running his world as he sees fit."

"And yours, too?" Bonnie sipped the sparkling wine appreciatively.

"Not really," Vicki said thoughtfully. "Oh, maybe in things like this." She waved an expressive hand over the table. "But not where it matters. He's incredibly generous, not just materially, but also emotionally. He makes many fewer demands on me than I do on him—probably too few," she added, a sudden frown creasing her brow. "The only thing he actually insists on is that I play 'president's wife' now and again."

"I should imagine that for you that's quite enough to be going on with?" Bonnie looked at her friend shrewdly.

Vicki shrugged. "I don't enjoy it. Occasionally, it conflicts with my work—then I yelp!" She laughed slightly.

"And how does Max cope with that?"

"With infinite patience, calm, and reason—it's quite infuriating sometimes. Let's order, shall we?" Vicki changed the subject, suddenly feeling that she had said enough.

A short silence fell after the flurry of choosing their meal. Bonnie broke it with her usual directness. "Regrets, Vicki?"

Vicki shook her head. "No, absolutely none at all," she declared with conviction. "But it's an odd business living with someone all the time. I'm still getting used to it."

Bonnie grinned slightly. "So, Vicki Carrolton-Randall, satisfy my curiosity by answering my original question. How did you find yourself in this exalted position? You were determined never to get married!"

"You haven't met Max yet." Vicki pulled off a leaf of her artichoke and dipped it in the accompanying vinaigrette dressing before sucking the juicy white meat from the base.

"Vicki, you're being remarkably evasive!"

"Oh, Lord, Bonnie!" She tossed the leaf into the bowl in front of her and pulled off another. "I'm not being evasive, it's just that I'm having to deal with it myself. Ever since I was ten, I've been announcing, 'I'll never be married.' I don't actually *feel* married most of the time now."

"Oh, that's rich, Vicki!" Bonnie laughed softly. "You had the East Coast society wedding of the year and you tell me you don't feel married! Even the Paris gossip columns carried the story. I can't remember the headlines exactly, but they were very lavish."

"That was *not* my idea," Vicki stated flatly. "Mother and Max cooked that one up, with the ample and forceful support of my dear brothers! I'd intended to have a quiet civil ceremony and let everyone know afterward. But everyone was against me. Max loves my family, and the feeling is mutual." She added mournfully, "I can handle one or the other of them, but not their combined forces."

"They must be some combination then," Bonnie said

matter-of-factly.

"You haven't met Max yet," Vicki repeated.

"How did *you* meet him? You said nothing in your letter about that, only a quick, apologetic statement that you were getting married."

"Was I apologetic? Yes, I suppose I was. It's hard to eat one's words, Bonnie, particularly when they've been stated so often and so unequivocally." She gave a small shrug. "Max just wouldn't take no for an answer. He doesn't understand how family closeness can be a problem some-times, never having had the dubious benefits of family life himself."

"How so?" Bonnie sat back to allow the waiter to remove her plate.

"His parents died when he was a baby. His grandfather raised him—or at least arranged for him to be raised by others. Max spent his early years in what amounted to a mausoleum, meeting his grandfather only for dinner, during which he was instructed in the duties and obligations of the heir to the Randall empire." Vicki smiled with gentle affec-tion. Remembering Max's quiet, matter-of-fact description of those lonely years filled her with sadness; so different from her own tempestuous upbringing as the only sister of three exuberant, domineering, but loving older brothers.

"Anyway," she continued briskly, "I suspect his longing for a family of his own lay behind this insistence on getting married. And I guess my protests weren't too convincing." She laughed softly. "To be honest, I was hooked from the first moment—I just resisted my feelings for a bit."

"You still haven't told me how you met," Bonnie per-sisted, examining her plate of broiled scallops with considerable enthusiasm.

"Oh, that! That was quite funny." Vicki chuckled at the memory. "You remember the small show I had at Astral when I was so mad because Dan insisted on exhibiting the self-portrait I did when Grandfather died?"

Bonnie nodded. "You wrote and told me all about the monumental row you'd had with Dan."

"Well, we compromised. Dan put an outrageous price on it, which we reckoned would put anyone off, but we *hadn't* reckoned on Max Randall's turning up! I suppose that in a way I was prepared to sell the picture, otherwise I wouldn't have agreed to putting *any* price on it, but it was still a part of me at that time. And while my pragmatic self was telling me I had a living to earn, my emotional self didn't want to sell this part of me. Am I making any sense?" She looked at Bonnie, who responded with a quick, accepting nod.

"Well, I was in the gallery at about five o'clock one evening, toward the end of the first week of the show—all the excitement was over and things had settled down. There was a steady stream of visitors attracted by the publicity, but nothing much more—you know what it's like. Dan was in the back, and suddenly this man appeared."

Her face softened at the memory, an expression not lost on Bonnie, who prompted her with a quiet, "Go on."

"Max walked in, and when I told him the gallery was about to close, he said, 'I'm aware of that, but I know exactly what I want.' He walked over to the portrait, looked at it, looked at me, and said, 'What the hell happened to you?' It was incredible, Bonnie! I found myself telling him all about Grandfather and that the portrait was not actually for sale. He just pointed out that it had a price on it and wrote out a check. Of course, Dan walked in right then, so Max stopped talking to me and just handed him the check. I grabbed it back and pushed it at Max and things went on like that for quite a while!"

"I can imagine." Bonnie was shaking with laughter.

"Well, eventually, I had to agree to sell the painting, and Max said he wanted it delivered to his apartment the next day. I got even more livid and said he couldn't possibly have it until the show closed, and he said he'd settle for that so long as the original would have dinner with him that night." Vicki shrugged. "I did, and the rest you know."

"You're right, Vicki. I have to meet this man." Bonnie sat back, heaving a sigh of satisfaction. "Anyone who provides Dom Pérignon for lunch deserves some attention!"

Vicki put her knife and fork together, regarding her friend closely. "Why don't you come and spend the evening with us? It's as hot as Hades outside; we can have a little cooler Westchester air, a swim, a quiet dinner on the patio. You can come into the city with Max in the morning, if you need to get back."

"That sounds good," Bonnie said enthusiastically. "I wasn't intending to work this afternoon anyway, but I have a full program of research at the Met to deal with tomorrow."

"Okay." Vicki beamed with pleasure. "Ivor, our next-door neighbor, is coming for dinner, too. His wife and kids are visiting family on the West Coast, so the poor soul's leading a miserable bachelor existence. You'll like him."

That settled, they sipped espresso while Bonnie brought Vicki up to date on her news. "Now," said Vicki when they had finished, an impish gleam in her green eyes, "watch this!" She beckoned to the hovering waiter and asked for the check. He disappeared, and within seconds the maître d' had replaced him at their table.

"Mr. Randall asked that your lunch be charged to his account, Mrs. Randall."

"I see." Vicki winked at Bonnie.

"Was everything quite satisfactory?"

"Perfectly, thank you," she replied, flashing him a warm smile as they rose from the table.

Once outside and away from the dignified observation of the restaurant staff, they both collapsed in a fit of schoolgirl giggles. "What did I tell you?" Vicki gasped. "And I bet you anything Max won't even mention it this evening."

"It's just so funny, Vicki, to imagine you allowing anyone to pay your way." Bonnie wiped her streaming eyes. "How do you manage your household finances?"

Vicki shrugged. "I never see any bills. I guess they're sent to the office and Lois, Max's secretary, pays them. She's been looking after the trivia of his life ever since he took over the company. I usually buy the food and see to my own needs. Max is always buying me clothes, but his taste is so superb I can hardly complain. Anyway, he likes to give things to people." She paused on the sidewalk, looking for a cab. "We had an early argument about my refusing to use his money. In the end, we compromised. I agreed to a joint account just in case I ever got into any trouble." She laughed. "Me in trouble, Bonnie! I got myself from one end of Europe to the other on the back of a motorcycle! But it makes Max happy, and I don't use it anyway."

Bonnie grinned as they got into the taxi. "Perhaps he doesn't know you too well yet."

"I'm not sure how well we know each other, actually," Vicki said thoughtfully.

Bonnie didn't respond, and Vicki was grateful for her friend's silence. She had already said much more than she had intended, but Bonnie was the only person to whom her usual reticence about her private life didn't apply. She was learning to reveal her innermost thoughts to Max, but it was a slow process. Still, Vicki reflected, she couldn't imagine her life now without Max. They shared so much already, and the rest would come in time. After all, Vicki told herself, after less than a year of marriage, a couple had to have *some* things to look forward to!

❧ 4 ❧

At Bonnie's hotel, Vicki lay on the bed reading her friend's latest article, as yet unpublished, while Bonnie threw a few things into a suitcase. They got into a lively discussion about Bonnie's projected book on Rembrandt, and it was with a gasp of horror that Vicki realized the time.

"It's five o'clock, the traffic will be horrendous, and I have to pick up something for dinner—I gave Josefa the day off! I can't leave poor Ivor waiting on the doorstep, and there's no knowing what time Max'll get away. We have to move, Bonnie!"

They hurried through the crowded streets toward Park Avenue. Vicki pushed through the swinging doors and into the lobby of the imposing building housing the New York offices of the Randall Corporation, briefly acknowledging the salute of the security guard before heading toward the elevator. Bonnie was close on her heels.

"Where are we going?" Bonnie asked breathlessly as the crowded elevator descended to the basement.

"My car," Vicki replied briefly. "We drove it in last night." Further explanations would have to wait. The elevator was packed with Randall Corporation employees, most of whom were aware that they were traveling with the president's wife, and she wasn't about to embarrass Max by giving a detailed description of their social life to such an interested audience.

Once in the underground garage, she headed for the space marked "Reserved for the President," where the sleek, low-slung Porsche stood.

"Wow," Bonnie breathed. "That is some car! It's exactly the color of your eyes."

Vicki laughed softly. "Max's idea of a birthday gift! Hop in, it's open." She pulled her keys from her purse, settling herself comfortably behind the wheel. She buckled her seat belt swiftly before turning the key in the ignition and putting the car into reverse. The powerful car moved out of the tight space, toward the exit.

"Good night, Mrs. Randall," the attendant called cheerfully.

" 'Night, Bill. Has Mr. Randall left yet?"

"Yes, about five minutes ago. Ed took him in the Rolls."

"That's a relief," Vicki declared, pulling out into the heavy traffic. "At least I don't have to worry about Ivor standing outside an empty house."

"Who's Ed?" Bonnie inquired.

"Max's chauffeur." Vicki shot her friend a quick grin. "Money has its uses, you know!"

"I never doubted it," Bonnie drawled. "The only thing

surprising me is how easily *you've* adapted!"

Silence fell as Vicki concentrated her attention on negotiating a path through the frenetic traffic. The two friends maintained the quiet until, at last, they were through Yonkers and onto the relatively empty Saw Mill River Parkway. Vicki put her foot down and the car sprang forward, purring like a jungle cat.

As the waiting policeman moved to the side of the road several hundred yards in front of her, jerking an imperative hand toward the shoulder, Victoria swore in soft, fluent Spanish.

"Trouble?" Bonnie asked as they pulled onto the hard shoulder ahead of the parked patrol car.

"Radar," Vicki muttered, winding down her window.

The officer stood by the car, feet planted firmly, well apart, notebook in hand. "You were doing sixty-nine miles per hour when you came into the straight after the corner."

In silence, Vicki handed over the required documents and sat fuming as he disappeared into his car. "I just don't believe it!" she exploded eventually. "Why do they *always* get me? It's this wretched car, Bonnie."

After what seemed a very long time, the officer reappeared. "You're going to be in trouble, lady," he said ponderously. "Another two points and you lose your license." He handed back her documents, then gave her the speeding ticket, which she signed with a resigned sigh, needing no further instruction. "You know, if you take my advice, you'll trade this in for something slower." He slapped the roof of the Porsche loudly, then returned to his car.

Vicki put the ticket on the dashboard before checking her rearview mirror and edging her way back onto the road, a scowl darkening her usually equable expression.

"Happens rather often, does it?" Bonnie asked prosaically, once they were moving smoothly again.

"You could say that," Victoria replied shortly. "I'm not the only person exceeding the speed limit around here, but you'd think so!"

"What's that dynamic husband of yours going to say?"

"Max? Oh, it's not his business," Vicki replied confidently. "He wouldn't even know about it, except that they keep bumping up the insurance premiums and he pays the insurance." She made a small pout. "I'm quite happy to pay the increase, so I can't see that it's any concern of his."

They stopped briefly at the supermarket in Croton village. Vicki, her usually sunny temper now restored, picked out fruit, vegetables, and steak with all the fastidiousness of a French housewife. A quick halt at the Italian bakery for a long loaf of bread and four cannolis, and they were on their way again, soon driving up the long, curved driveway toward the Randalls' sprawling white house.

The front door opened as Vicki cut the engine, and Max, wearing only a pair of denim shorts, loped easily toward the car. Vicki wound down the window, lifting her face toward the sun of his smile and the firm pressure of his lips on hers.

"Meet Bonnie, Max." She smiled.

"Hello, Bonnie." He stretched a hand through the window in greeting. Then his eye caught the slip on the dash. "Oh, Victoria, not again!" He examined it with a quick shake of his head. "Sixty-nine miles per hour, for godsake!"

"It's this car," she protested with a laugh. "It doesn't know how to go slowly."

"Tell that to the judge!" With a swift movement, Max

removed the keys from the ignition and pocketed them, before opening the door for her. "Come on, I've made margaritas. Ivor's inside."

Vicki scrambled out of the car, running to catch up with him as he strode across the gravel, toward the house. "Hey! What have you done with my keys?"

"You're grounded, Victoria," he called back over his shoulder.

"You can't *do* that to me, Max. Wait up!"

"I just did," he said cheerfully, patting her keys in his back pocket but slowing down for her.

Bonnie caught up with them, convulsed with laughter. "I thought you said it was none of his business, Vicki."

"It's not!" Vicki insisted. "Max, stop playing games. I insist that you give me back my keys."

"Oh, I will," he said equably, "but not until the end of next week. After you." He held the door for her with a gently mocking bow. Vicki marched past him, shooting a furious look from beneath her arched eyebrows.

"Ivor, do you believe this?" Vicki strode into the kitchen, too infuriated to greet her guest properly. "Max has decided to play macho man. He's taken away my car keys just because I got a speeding ticket!"

"Not *a* speeding ticket," Max corrected her mildly. "About the sixth in as many months."

Ivor Kuzinski uncurled his lean, angular frame from an elegant chrome-legged chair at the teak breakfast table. "I hate to say it, Vicki dear, but at this point he's merely anticipating the court."

"Max is exaggerating!" Vicki, with difficulty, refrained from stamping her foot and attempted to moderate her tone.

"Look, if I get my license suspended, that's my problem, okay?"

"My love, I don't think you realize quite how much of a problem that would be. If you spend a week without wheels, you just might. Here." Max handed her a shallow, salt-encrusted glass of clear liquid. "At the rate you're going, by the end of the month you'll be without keys for a lot longer than a few days!"

Taking a slow sip of her drink, Vicki decided to change her tactics. "I don't think we should argue any more in front of our guests. But don't imagine you've heard the last of this, Max Randall." With that, she dropped the subject and introduced Bonnie and Ivor to each other. Then, picking up the pitcher of margaritas, Vicki ushered her guests outside onto the patio, dropping with a sigh of relief onto the cushioned seat of a wrought-iron chair at the parasol-shaded table.

"That pool looks very inviting," Bonnie remarked after a while. "You promised me a swim, Vicki."

"I could do with one, too." Vicki put her glass down and got to her feet. "Your things are in the trunk." She held out her hand to Max. "If you'll just give me the keys . . ."

Max shook his head. "Nice try, green eyes." Amusement bubbled in his voice. "But I'll bring them in; although you've obviously conveniently forgotten that you can open the trunk from inside the car."

Vicki pulled a face, but having decided not to argue at this point, she linked her arm through Bonnie's and drew her friend back into the house. "Let me give you the tour," she said cheerfully. They walked through the spacious, elegant house while Bonnie, nodding appreciatively, examined the furniture in the many-windowed living room, the huge, heavy mahogany table in the dining room easily accommodating twelve place settings, the richness of the Oriental rugs scattered in seemingly careless fashion over the highly polished floors.

"You and Max seem to share the same tastes," she observed.

Vicki laughed and nodded. "In everything, including food." She led her friend upstairs to the three-sided gallery overlooking the central hall. "Before I show you the bedrooms, come see my studio."

They went through a fireproof door and up a flight of wooden stairs to the third floor. A huge room ran the length and breadth of the back of the house. The north-facing wall was all double-glazed window, and an enormous skylight took up the central portion of the ceiling.

"Isn't it marvelous?" Vicki grinned at her friend's stupefied expression. "It was Max's wedding gift. Just after we bought the house, he introduced me to this fantastic architect and said, 'Go create the perfect studio.' We had such fun, Bonnie, you can't imagine!" She began to prance around the room, flicking on spot lights, demonstrating the elaborate system of shading for the windows. "I've never had such a perfect workplace. The lighting took months to get right."

Bonnie grinned. "As usual, there's not a single Vicki Carrolton canvas on display."

Vicki looked around the room—every painting was either covered or faced the wall. Even the easel, carrying the third of the holocaust series, was facing away from the door. She shrugged. *"Plus ça change, plus c'est la même chose,*

Bonnie. You can look if you want to."

"Another time, Vicki," her friend responded easily. "You don't have time to show me properly right now. I wouldn't mind a quick peep at the holocaust series though."

Vicki, without a word, went across the orderly, workman-like room, turned two canvases away from the wall, and lifted their shrouds. "The third is on the easel; it's not going well," she explained.

Bonnie prowled around the paintings, her thick eyebrows drawn fiercely together. After a while, she dropped the sheets over the canvases again and placed a gentle arm over Vicki's shoulders. "It's one thing to write about other people's work, kid, quite another to produce the originals. They're very disturbing."

"Supposed to be," Vicki responded briefly. "That's the main problem with the third one. I can feel the desolation, but it's so powerful I think I'm scared to paint it as I feel it."

"Come along, Victoria, out of here! I thought you two were going to have a swim." Max stood in the doorway. They hadn't heard the quiet footsteps on the stairs, and Vicki turned sharply at the soft but resolute voice.

"So we are. I just wanted to show Bonnie my studio."

"You've done so. If you stay up here any longer, we may as well forget all thoughts of a relaxed social evening." He crossed the room, his smile softening the words as he pinched her cheek.

"Okay, Svengali." She smiled back. "We're on our way."

Vicki shut the door firmly behind her, following the others down to the second floor. Max was right, of course. If she began to get involved in a discussion of her work, she would become so wrapped up in the subject that she would forget all else.

"I put Bonnie's things in the guest room," Max called over his shoulder. "Ivor and I are going to swim. Don't keep us waiting too long!"

"Strong willed, that husband of yours," Bonnie commented casually as she looked appreciatively around the comfortable, well-appointed guest room.

Vicki chuckled softly. "That's a fairly accurate description. What's so peculiar is that he doesn't actually *impose* his will on anyone; people just seem to do what he wants automatically, without even being aware of it. I've never heard him raise his voice; he just . . . sort of ignores the opposition," she finished with a slight, puzzled shake of the head. She was no more immune than anyone else to this quality of her husband's.

"Well, he certainly gave the impression that he intends to impose his will about that car of yours." Bonnie began to unpack, searching for her swimsuit in the small suitcase.

Vicki walked over to the window. She looked down at the pool and patio beneath. Max and Ivor were in the water, racing against each other with the dogged single-mindedness that characterized them both. They weren't really enjoying themselves, she decided. Exercising was just one of those things that had to be done if you spent too many hours of the day behind a desk. She turned back to Bonnie with a soft laugh.

"Oh, I think he's just playing games. I'll sort him out later. He may be assertive, but he's no tyrant!" She looked seriously at Bonnie. "You know, Max has as many women in top positions in the corporation as he has men."

"He treats women just the same as men, does he?" Bonnie

quirked a disbelieving eyebrow.

"No! That's exactly my point," Vicki stated firmly. "As far as Max is concerned, women are different—not better or worse than men, just different. They see things differently, behave differently, but that in no way detracts from their skills and abilities. In fact, it actually adds to them. Sure, he expects me to charm and soften up an occasional difficult business opponent for him, but he reckons that's just using a skill that I have. I don't feel bad about doing it. At least," she added frankly, "not *too* bad." She ducked as Bonnie hurled a cushion at her.

"Whatever has happened to the feisty Vicki Carrolton?"

"She grew up," Vicki replied with a laugh. "One can't play *enfant terrible* forever. I got that out of my system during those years in Europe. Would you believe that Mother and I are getting on rather well at the moment?"

"No, I wouldn't," Bonnie declared. "Max is clearly a miracle worker. Are you intending to swim in your clothes, naked, or in a suit? Because I'm ready."

"Go on down, I'll be with you in two minutes." Vicki went off to her own bedroom, a slight smile curving her lips. Only to Bonnie could she put the half-formed ideas into words. She knew that her friend would hear what she was trying to say and would somehow make sense of it without ever losing her light touch or crossing the sensitive boundaries of Vicki's privacy.

Slipping into the deep-pink bikini that accentuated her tan and left little of her figure to the imagination, Vicki made her way outside. Max swung his legs out of the pool where he was sitting on the edge talking to Bonnie and rose fluidly to his feet.

"Come on, speed demon." He laughed. "Get in the water before I throw you in!"

"You'd like that, wouldn't you?" she bantered, her eyes gleaming as she saw his responsive glint.

"Yes, I would." Catching her up by the waist, he swung her body easily away from him, slipping one arm under her knees. "Now," he whispered, "hold tight."

Vicki put her arms firmly around Max's neck as he walked with her to the end of the diving board, reveling in the sensuous feel of his bare flesh against hers. Balancing lightly, toes curled over the edge of the board, Max grinned down at her. "I wish I were making love to you right now." Her eyes danced responsively as he jumped neatly into the water, his arms tightening around her as they went under. Vicki controlled the instinctive response to kick upward as the blue surface closed over her head, instead allowing herself to meld into Max's strong body as they sank to the bottom. Max pushed upward as his feet hit the tiled floor, releasing her with a swift push when they broke into sunlight again.

Gasping, laughing, Vicki swam away from him. After several lengths, she hitched herself onto the patio with an agile twist of her body. Max, still dripping, was tending the coals in the brick barbecue pit. Vicki went to stand beside him and rested her wet head against his shoulder, suddenly realizing that they were alone.

Max put the tongs down and turned her to face him, running one hand through her wet hair, while he draped the other arm across her shoulder. "Did you enjoy your lunch, little love?" One finger moved to caress her eyelid.

"Yes, thank you," Vicki replied with a ridiculous attempt

at a prim curtsy. "I had rather expected to pay for it myself, though."

"My pleasure, golden girl." He laughed gently. "Go get dry—the sun's going down. You can pay for your lunch by cooking dinner."

"Oh, no," she said firmly. "I'll make the salad, you cook the steaks. Fair exchange?"

"I guess so, but I want *you* to put a shirt on, right now!"

"Okay, okay, bossy! I hope you don't assume that you can brave the night air without protection yourself?"

For answer, Max picked up a beach robe from a nearby lounge and slung it around his shoulders. "Satisfied?" he questioned with a grin.

Victoria inclined her head in a quick, expressive gesture of acceptance before going toward the pool house in search of towels and a shirt.

"Here." Ivor, who was rubbing his head vigorously with one hand, tossed her a thick towel as she walked in. "Time for another margarita, I think. Bonnie and I will go do something about it."

Vicki nodded cheerfully. "Be with you in a minute."

"Mmm, I feel good." Vicki heaved a sensuous sigh of satisfaction, and leaned back in her chair, her feet twining themselves around Max's legs under the table. "I can't stand the thought of winter, and having to spend all that time inside, huddled in front of a log fire."

"Oh, I don't know," Ivor said idly, sipping his coffee. "I'm looking forward to finding my skis and ice skates again."

"I suppose there's always that." Vicki pinched the citronella candle on the table, controlling the flow of wax between thumb and forefinger. "But there's also the prospect of a family Thanksgiving and Christmas, not to mention living in the city after the first of the year."

Max shot her a look that visibly puzzled their companions, and Vicki chewed her lip in annoyance. She hadn't intended to mar the relaxed atmosphere by bringing up that particular bone of contention. She didn't want to move into their city apartment for the winter, but Max had been quietly adamant that he couldn't risk being snowbound in Westchester and, anyway, they would have a lot of necessary social and business engagements during the winter that would make commuting difficult. Vicki had agreed reluctantly, biting off the need to tell him that she wouldn't be able to work properly away from her beloved studio. But she had only been postponing the inevitable confrontation—partly out of cowardice, she admitted to herself reluctantly, and partly out of her firm belief that there was no point anticipating trouble.

There was trouble aplenty later that evening! As soon as they reached the privacy of their bedroom, Vicki tackled Max, with the utmost confidence of success, on the issue of the car. She discovered, to her utter amazement, that he was serious. A dismissive shake of his head was his only response to her protests.

"Look, Max, this is absolutely ridiculous. You're treating me as if I were an irresponsible teenager." Vicki forced a note of reason into her voice, standing, arms akimbo, barring his way to the bathroom.

"I'm doing you a favor, Victoria," he replied evenly. "In fact, I'm doing both of us a favor. I don't fancy having you housebound or dependent on public transportation for months!"

"That is my decision, not yours." Powerful anger was rising slowly within her, but she put it on hold. It was a last-resort weapon and one she had never used with Max before.

"Don't glare at me like that, green eyes. You can use cabs and the train for a week—sure, it'll be inconvenient, but I'm just asking you to experience that inconvenience for a very short while." His tone was patient, amused even, and Vicki realized that he had no idea how close she was to unleashing her anger.

"You are not *asking* me, you're *telling* me," she said icily. "People stopped telling me what to do a long time ago."

"That just may have been a mistake!" Max laughed affectionately. "Come on, Victoria. We'll compromise—just three days. Try it for me." He moved toward her, still laughing, but both the movement and the laughter were a mistake.

With quiet deliberation, Vicki let herself go, expressing her outrage in a fluent stream and in a variety of languages, but the point was most clearly stated in her narrowed, furious eyes and rigid body. A look of total, bewildered disbelief crossed Max's face.

"Good Lord, Victoria!" He put his hands on her shoulders. "Stop it, please!" Touching her was another error, and did nothing to stem the flow of her invective.

For a second, he was stunned. Then, without a word, he seized both her wrists in one large hand and, jerking her arms high above her head, pushed her backward until the edge of the platform caught her behind the knees and she fell onto the wide mattress. Still holding her wrists, Max proceeded to sit at the head of the bed, patiently prepared to wait it out.

He didn't have long to wait. Vicki had never believed in wasting energy, and expressing outrage, however legitimate, at the ceiling was a singularly unsatisfactory activity.

"Would you let me go, please?" Her voice was now quiet and completely calm.

"With pleasure," Max replied levelly. "But I want your promise that you've stopped yelling."

"You have it."

He released her immediately, getting to his feet and quietly continuing his preparations for bed.

Vicki sat up slowly, peering at her wrists. His hold had been so gentle that they showed not the slightest redness; she was denied even the satisfaction of rubbing them reproachfully! Stripping off her now-dry swimsuit, she got into bed, pulled the covers up to her chin, and rested against the piled-up pillows, a thoughtful frown creasing her brow. She very rarely lost her temper these days, even with her equally volatile family or with Dan, but when it did happen, a quick shouting match ensued that almost always ended in laughter and compromise. But Max had reacted in the most extraordinary way—he had refused to enter the battle and had just immobilized her; simple, but very effective!

Max crossed the oak floor from the bathroom and dropped onto the bed. He drew the covers up over his long, lean nakedness. "Sulking, green eyes?" He turned sideways, regarding her steadily.

"No, I never sulk," Vicki replied. "I'm just regrouping."

Max gave a short laugh. "Tell me, Victoria, how often can I expect to be treated to displays of that kind?"

"Oh, you needn't worry," she said calmly. "I don't waste that weapon on people who don't appreciate it, and it's clearly lost on you."

"That's good." Max hitched himself up against the pillows. "Because I'm not sure I could behave with such restraint another time."

Vicki sat up, hugging her knees, resting her head against them with her face turned away from Max. "Did I shock you?" she inquired softly. "I'm sorry if I did."

"Don't do it again—okay?"

"I'll try not to," Vicki replied, sucking in her bottom lip.

"You'll have to do better than try, Victoria," Max stated bluntly.

Silence fell in the dimly lit room. Vicki was more shaken than she cared to admit and suspected that the quiet figure beside her was also trying to absorb what had just happened. The issue itself seemed no longer important, but the naked, raw emotion it had created left them both feeling drained.

Max broke the silence. They still hadn't touched each other. "Just how long could you have carried on with that stream of fury without repeating yourself?" There was genuine interest in his voice.

"Oh, a very long time—I just switch languages when my vocabulary runs out. Being able to swear in the vernacular is a very useful skill."

"Is it?" he queried, eyebrows raised in disbelief.

"It's saved me a great many necessary pennies on occasion, and once or twice even my skin!" Vicki told him firmly.

"Well, since you don't have to worry about either of those

things with me, I assume you'll save that particular tool for when I'm not around?"

She nodded quietly, laying a hand on his arm. "I'm sorry, Max, but you angered me."

Long fingers grasped her chin, turning her face toward his. "I'm not scared of your anger, Victoria. I just don't like it!"

Vicki sucked in her breath sharply—there was a cold finality in his words that took all the games-playing aspect out of her behavior—and it was, to a large extent, a game. The entire Carrolton family yelled and fought, never expecting anyone to take the angry words to heart. Battles were over and resolved as quickly as they began. She had always behaved like that, and no one, before Max, had treated her tantrums with such deadly seriousness.

"Let's sleep." He flicked the light switch near the bed and drew her against him as they slid down under the covers. His arm held her quietly, passively, her head resting in the hollow of his shoulder; but there was no sense of togetherness. Vicki moved a tentative hand across Max's concave belly, running a finger around the indentation of his navel.

"Not tonight, Victoria." He pushed her hand away firmly but gently.

"My family has one very good principle," she said softly. "We never let the sun go down on our anger. You're still angry, Max."

In the following quiet, she resumed her gentle stroking and fingering, feeling his body stir beneath her light, tantalizing touch. When he made no further protest, she began to love him with her lips, tongue, and hands, moving sinuously across his flesh until he turned on his side.

"Come here, wife," he murmured in her ear, flipping her

onto her side to face him. With a sigh of relief, she flung a leg across his hips as he pulled her tightly against his body and slipped inside her. They moved with gentle, rhythmic, healing strokes. They loved softly, tenderly, reaching a quiet peace in the calm darkness and the soft, nesting warmth under the blanketing covers.

❦ 5 ❦

"Wake up, sleepyhead." The insistent hand on her shoulder was forcing her into wakefulness. Vicki rolled over, burying her face in the pillow, fighting to regain the blissful unconsciousness. "Come along, Victoria. You have a guest, remember? You must at least *offer* breakfast!"

With a deep sigh, Vicki released the pillow, rolling onto her back, gazing with sleepy eyes at the amused face above her.

"Drink your orange juice; it'll bring you back to the land of the living," Max cajoled, laughing.

She hitched herself onto one elbow, drinking greedily of the sharp, clean-tasting liquid and watching Max pad methodically around the room. "There ought to be a law against this," Vicki muttered.

"Against what?" Max grinned.

"Against people like you bouncing around like spring lambs at such an ungodly hour!"

Max gave a shout of laughter. "Get your act together, now. I want to leave in half an hour."

Vicki pushed off the covers and stood, digging her feet into the deep, luxurious pile of the carpet. She stretched, yawned, and welcomed the new sun-bright day. Max pulled a robe out of her closet, tossing it across to her.

"Thanks." Vicki shrugged herself into the soft garment and made her way to the dresser. "I'd better go wake Bonnie." She began to tug a hairbrush through her tousled mass of red-gold hair.

"I already did," Max said coolly. "She was considerably more polite and appreciative of her glass of orange juice than some I could mention!"

Vicki grinned at him. "You knew exactly what I'm like in the morning before we got married."

"And you, my love, knew exactly what *I'm* like," Max came back swiftly.

"Fair enough," Vicki agreed. "What do you want for breakfast?"

"Scrambled eggs and bacon."

"That's obscene!" She shot him a frown and made for the door.

"Oh, Victoria? Catch!"

Vicki spun around, instinctively moving into the position her brothers had so painstakingly taught her, deftly receiving the key ring as it flew through the air.

"I love to see you do that." Max chuckled, turning back to the mirror, beginning to knot his tie. "I've never seen you miss a throw yet."

"Tom used to box my ears every time I dropped a catch. You learn quickly under those circumstances!" She laughed back.

"Funny, I can't imagine Tom bullying you," Max observed thoughtfully.

"Oh, he didn't!" Vicki responded, thinking of her adored oldest brother. "He never hurt me, just used to stand there with a look of total exasperation on his face saying, 'Just because you're a girl, infant, doesn't mean you can't catch a ball!'" She looked at the keys in her palm, and asked softly, "Had a change of heart, Max?"

"No. I fully intended to give them back to you this morning. I just wanted to make a point." Max turned from the mirror and their eyes met.

"Well, you certainly did that," Vicki said emphatically.

"As I remember, we both did," Max responded dryly, picking up his jacket.

"I think we learned a few things about each other that we didn't know before," she said gravely.

"What did you learn?" He looked fixedly at her.

"That you are actually capable of anger," Vicki said simply. "But not my kind—yours is cold and a lot more scary."

"That, Victoria, is why I avoid losing my temper. In my family, anger has caused a great deal of heartache."

"I see." Vicki left the room, turning over his words as she made her barefoot way to the kitchen; he was going to have to tell her about that. She opened the glass doors onto the patio, letting in the fresh, early-morning air before mea-suring coffee into the electric pot and plugging it into the outlet.

"What a gorgeous morning!" Bonnie bounced cheerfully into the kitchen.

"Isn't it?" Vicki concurred readily. "Max wants eggs and bacon, how about you?"

"Just toast and coffee, thanks," Bonnie replied, going over to the open doors. "Can we eat outside?"

"Sure. Do you want to grab some silverware? Left-hand

drawer under the sink." Vicki deftly broke eggs into a bowl, whisking them quickly as she checked the bacon on the grill.

Max appeared in the kitchen, briskly dumping his briefcase on the table. "I'm just going to—"

"Check the telex," Vicki finished for him. They both laughed, and Bonnie turned slowly toward her, a handful of knives and forks in her hand, as Max left the room.

"You know, Vicki, I think I approve of this marriage of yours," she said consideringly.

"So do I," Vicki replied cheerfully, "but don't tell Jean-Pierre, he'll never believe you!"

Bonnie chuckled softly. "He'd certainly never believe you could be so good-tempered in the morning."

"Who couldn't?" Max appeared in the doorway, scanning the print-out in his hand with an intense frown.

"Jean-Pierre," Vicki informed him matter-of-factly. "He used to camp out in our apartment when he was destitute, which was actually rather often."

"Poor Jean-Pierre! I can't imagine coping with you in the morning, unless there were compensations," Max teased, standing behind her, running a long finger over her neck as she neatly turned the perfectly cooked eggs onto buttered toast, surrounding them with rashers of bacon.

"Jean-Pierre's preferences don't include women," Vicki stated with a laugh, handing him the plate. "We were, as they say, just good friends!"

Max tweaked her nose as he took his breakfast. "As you know, my love, I'm not concerned about your activities before I met you. It's what you do now that's of interest to me."

"Perhaps I should eat my toast somewhere else," Bonnie murmured, "if you two are about to have an intimate discussion about Vicki's sinful past."

"Sit down, Bonnie," Max ordered with a grin. "As I just said, I have no intention of discussing Victoria's past, now or at any other time."

"What sinful past? I should have been so lucky!" Vicki rejoined, pouring coffee into thick china mugs. "Oh, by the way—" she carried the mugs outside, putting them on the white wrought-iron table—"I invited Dan and Bev for lunch on Sunday. Dan wants to see how the 'holocaust' is doing. I hope this visit doesn't conflict with anything?" She raised her eyebrows at Max over the rim of her mug—usually she checked with him first before issuing invitations. However, he simply shook his head, his mouth too full of bacon to respond verbally.

"Good," Vicki said with satisfaction. "Why don't you come, too, Bonnie? You can't have seen Dan in years."

"I haven't," Bonnie replied, spooning thick honey onto her toast. "And I'd love to come, thanks."

An amicable silence fell for a while until Max frowned and cocked his head. "I hear Ed with the car. Are you nearly ready, Bonnie?"

Bonnie went off to get her suitcase, and Max sat back in his chair, patting his lap with a gesture that was both a demand and an invitation. Victoria smiled and went over to him, allowing him to pull her down to him. "I'll get home early tonight," he said softly. "We have a few things to say to each other, I think."

"I guess so," Vicki agreed hesitantly. "It's just that you seem to take our spat so much more seriously than I do."

"Evidently, I do." He held her upright on his knee, squinting at her against the rosy ball of the morning sun. "You don't think that's worth discussing?"

"Yes, of course I do. It's just rather new for me. You couldn't just forget it, I suppose?" Vicki looked at him wistfully.

" 'Fraid not, my love." Max set her firmly on her feet. "I have to make some sense of it, otherwise it'll just fester." He touched the tip of her nose with a light forefinger. "One thing, though . . ."

"Well?" Vicki queried.

"When you do lose your driver's license, don't expect me to put a chauffeur-driven car at your disposal!" Max laughed at her indignant expression, silencing her expostulation with a quick, hard kiss. "Come see me off."

Vicki watched the car until it turned out of sight at the end of the driveway, then she began to walk barefoot across the dew-laden grass, toward the back of the house. Today she needed to be quite alone, to sort out the confusion that last night's scene had created and to prepare herself for this evening. She had never been scared of confronting her emotions any more than she was scared of expressing them. Anger was as valid an emotion as love, and if Max had such difficulty with it, that was going to cause problems—they couldn't expect always to live in an idyll where all was sweetness and light. She certainly wouldn't be able to paint in that sort of emotional desert. Pain, fear, desolation, anger, loss—these were her subject matter; not exclusively, of course, but her best work was informed by them.

Within an hour she was in the kitchen, making herself a fat sandwich, which she slung with a couple of cans of beer and her sketch pad into a backpack.

Josefa was crossing the driveway from her apartment over the garage as Vicki ran lightly out of the front door. "Morning, Josefa," she called cheerfully. "I've left you a note on the kitchen table about dinner." The housekeeper raised a hand in smiling acknowledgment, and Victoria wheeled her bicycle out of the garage, humming softly as she pedaled briskly down the drive and turned toward the river.

It was early evening when, tired, sun soaked, and at peace, she came home. The Rolls stood, gleaming dully, in front of the house. That meant that either Max had driven himself home or Ed was having a drink and a chat with Josefa.

"Where were you?" Max stood in the doorway as she plodded with the pleasurable weariness of physical fatigue across the drive from the garage.

"By the river, mostly." Vicki smiled up at him. "I'm sorry. I meant to be here when you got back, but I didn't realize how early 'early' was going to be!"

"No matter." He ran a finger down her freckled nose, stroking the mobile mouth with a frown of concentration. "You're all grubby and sweaty." Max laughed softly, picking grass out of her hair, wiping her damp forehead with his handkerchief.

"If you'll let me get to the shower, I could do something about it." Vicki grinned. "Just dusting me off isn't going to do the trick."

"I guess not—you're a hopeless case! You're such a tomboy, Victoria!" Flinging a careless arm around the slim, bare shoulders revealed by her halter-neck shirt, he propelled her into the house. "Give me that." He gestured toward her backpack as they reached the foot of the stairs. "I'll take it into the kitchen and unpack it while you clean yourself up."

"Be careful of my sketch pad." Victoria handed it over. "I've had rather a productive day—see what you think."

Max was sitting at the patio table, examining her day's work, when Vicki joined him. She was shining with health and cleanliness, enjoying the cool, sensuous touch of her light cotton shift as it swung against the bare skin beneath.

"What do you think?" She sat opposite him, sipping the glass of white wine waiting for her on the table.

"Well, I think if this is what goes on in public places in Westchester, it shouldn't be allowed!" Max shook his head at her in amazement, and she gave a low chuckle.

"They actually had their clothes on—I just took them off for my own purposes." Rising, she went to look over his shoulder, examining the two naked, entwined figures sharply delineated on the sketch pad. "It's not supposed to be lascivious . . ." Vicki frowned. "I was trying to capture that naive, ingenuous quality they had—so much in love, but so unsure; a couple of kids not really knowing what to do next but feeling that they should know." She shrugged. "Perhaps it's not so good."

"Idiot." Max put a hand around her waist, squeezing her tightly. "You know damn well it's good—it encapsulates a whole period of one's life. They're so vulnerable, yet so brave."

"I'm glad you can see it," she said simply.

"Would you like me to serve dinner, Mrs. Randall?" Josefa appeared on the patio, but Vicki shook her head swiftly.

"No thanks, Josefa, that's fine. We're not ready to eat just yet. Why don't you go home now?"

"Whatever you say. The crabs are all dressed and in the refrigerator, and the veal is ready for the pan. The asparagus just needs to be steamed," Josefa said efficiently. "I made bread this afternoon—there's a fresh loaf in the bread drawer."

"You're a marvel." Vicki smiled at her. "See you Wednesday."

"If you're sure you don't need me tomorrow?" the house-keeper said doubtfully.

"Quite sure," Vicki assured her cheerfully. "Have a good one."

Max shook his head gently as the woman disappeared. "You know, Victoria, we pay Josefa an enormous salary, but you hardly use her at all."

She shrugged dismissively. "I really don't want someone around all the time. I'm quite capable of cooking and shopping myself, Max."

"When you're not working, yes," he agreed. "But what about all those times when you can't even talk to anyone, let alone think about housekeeping?"

"That's why we have Josefa," Vicki stated reasonably. "But since now is not one of those times, why should we sacrifice our privacy? It suits both Josefa and me very well. She pulls out all the stops when I'm otherwise occupied."

"I guess so." Max sighed. "It's just not what I'm used to."

"Poor love, do I really make you suffer that much?" She slid her arms around his neck, nibbling his ear gently.

"You did last night," Max responded quietly.

"Oh." Victoria straightened up and returned to her chair. "I suppose it's time to talk about that now?"

Max nodded gravely. "Do you want to tell me what happened, or shall I start?"

"Whichever," Vicki said quietly.

"You, then." He refilled their glasses and sat back, waiting.

"I'm not going to be able to apologize any more than I did last night," Vicki said slowly.

"I'm not asking for apologies, just an explanation," he rejoined firmly.

"It's hard to know quite where to start." Vicki frowned into her glass. "I don't know whether to explain my attitude about anger or tell you why I became so angry."

"Start with the why."

"You didn't have the right to behave like that," she said bluntly. "What I do with my life is my business. You were highhanded and invaded my space. While I thought you were playing a game, I wasn't angry, but then you convinced me that you were serious."

"Then you don't accept that what you do also affects me?" Max asked quietly.

"Yes, of course I do, but I don't accept your right to control what I do. No one has that right," Vicki added forcefully. "Naturally, my activities, my thoughts . . . oh, everything about me in some way impinges on your life." Victoria looked at him in some frustration. "How can I explain that while I acknowledge *that* fact, I don't give you the right to direct what I do? I have to follow my own path, darling. I don't intend that it should adversely affect you, Max, but now and again it's going to." His face was still and quiet across the table, showing nothing, giving her no help as she struggled to find the right words.

"Look," Vicki resumed, "you and I are not going to be able to live in perpetual harmony and peace. It's impossible for any two people to do so, and we can't live in each other's pockets either. That business with the car was trivial and unimportant except that it made a point."

"So, if I see you on a collision course, you're saying I may not intervene?"

"Basically, yes; that *is* what I'm saying."

"But your welfare is my concern," Max said simply.

"And so is yours mine, but I'm not going to interfere in your choice as to how you live your life. We're different people, Max. And marriage gives neither partner any absolute rights over the other."

"Who's talking about rights, Victoria?" A note of impatience crept into his voice. "I'm talking about two people who each voluntarily yield some of their independence and their space, as you put it, in exchange for support, love, and friendship."

Vicki nodded slowly. "I can't argue with that, intellectually, but you've never had to fight your way out of a close family circle—to say to people who love you and whom you love, 'Leave me alone, I don't belong to you or to anyone.' Have you?"

"No!" There was pain in his eyes, and she longed to comfort him, but couldn't until she had explained.

"Look, Max. Tom, Steve, Mike, and I are as close as any group of siblings can be. They practically raised me!" She laughed softly. "Poor mother was so shocked at finding herself pregnant again when her youngest child was twelve, and then giving birth to a girl of all things, that I don't think she ever recovered. That left my brothers with a free hand. Father was always too busy to do much more than make decisions about what schools I should attend and that sort of thing. My brothers took me on as if I were some sort of holy mission! Until I left home, they seemed to control every aspect of my life. They always loved me, certainly, but sometimes love can be smothering."

"Don't you think you're exaggerating just a bit?" Max asked, a deep frown drawing his thick eyebrows together.

"No!" Vicki responded vigorously. "I'm not. That's why I had to go away. I lived a fairly crazy existence for ten years, but I found myself in the process and became a real painter," she added softly. "I need space, Max. I make my own mistakes, my own decisions, and no one, not even you, is going to take that away from me."

"I don't want to, Victoria," Max said quietly. "But I love you."

Vicki sighed and then tried again. "Sometimes loving people means enduring the pain of letting go, sometimes even watching them hurt themselves."

Max was silent for long minutes, gazing into his glass. Intellectually, he could see her point just as she could see his, but it didn't seem to help somehow. "Well, I suppose you've explained fairly clearly why you got angry," he said at last. "I can't promise that I won't behave that way again. It's not in my nature to let something happen that I can prevent."

"I suppose I've always known that," Vicki said slowly, "and I'll try to understand." Paradoxically, it was just this quality in him that she had always found particularly compelling. She regarded him steadily. "It's your turn now. Why do you avoid anger?"

"Randall anger is rather different from the Carrolton version," he began slowly. "It's slow burning, cold, and, as you said this morning, scary. There are branches of my family that are in their second generation of not speaking to each other."

"What?" Victoria exclaimed. It was impossible to imagine anything like that happening in her family. Sure, they said hurtful things to each other in moments of rage, but a cold refusal to speak to each other afterward was inconceivable.

"If my grandfather had been prepared to communicate with my uncle, I might have had a much less lonely childhood," Max went on matter-of-factly. "I have a host of cousins that I never met until Grandfather's funeral. My aunt repeatedly invited me for the holidays, but I was never allowed to go."

"Oh, Lord," Vicki said softly, filled with horror at the chasm of loneliness revealed by his words. "My poor love." She moved swiftly around the table. "No wonder you were so upset last night. Max—I'll try to prevent a repeat episode—at least over something so trivial," she amended.

"I'll try, too, my love. You'll just have to tell me when I seem to be controlling. It's quite unconscious; I'll just have to learn to recognize it."

"I suppose you couldn't learn ordinary anger, as well?" She ran her fingers through his hair, smiling slightly sadly into his eyes.

"I don't know how," he replied bluntly, pushing up her long skirt and beginning slowly to caress her, stroking and kneading the firm, slim thighs and the soft roundness of her hips. Vicki stretched luxuriantly, arching the small of her back against his hands. Max stood up, lifting the dress over her head as he did so.

"Max, what if someone comes," she whispered as he led her firmly over to the rich green lawn bordering the patio.

"That's their problem," he said softly, pulling her down as he stripped off his shorts. "It's a consequence of invading other people's privacy."

Privacy, Vicki thought before all coherent thought left her, perhaps that was what this was all about. But how on earth did one manage to respect and maintain each partner's privacy while simultaneously living in the most intimate of close quarters? There had to be a way, she decided in the swirling, sun-shot depths behind her closed eyes as her body flew upward into the vastnesses of deep blue space— it was simply a question of finding it.

❦ 6 ❦

Vicki left Dan's gallery, a thoughtful frown creasing her brow. It was another muggy, humid August day, and she was forcibly aware of how much she hated New York in the summer. She didn't particularly care for it in the winter, either, she reflected. City life stifled her; the air and the quality of the light somehow left her insufficient freedom to think creatively. But the morning had not been wasted— those bronze statuettes were quite beautiful and, unless she was much mistaken, would be a very good investment.

The lobby of the Randall Corporation building was pleasantly cool, and the private elevator whisked her with smooth rapidity to the president's suite. Lois looked up from her typewriter with a warm smile.

"Good morning, Mrs. Randall. How are you today?"

"Hot," Vicki replied with a grin. "Is his lordship free?" She gestured with her head toward the door leading to Max's inner sanctum.

Lois laughed. It had taken her quite a while to get used to Vicki's blithe irreverence when referring to the president. "Mr. Hudson is with him, but I don't think you'd be interrupting anything too important." She pushed the intercom button.

"Yes, Lois." Max's quiet, courteous voice came across.

"Your wife is here, Mr. Randall."

"That's nice." Max chuckled softly. "Come on in, Victoria."

The enormous, elegant office was cool, bars of sunlight crossing the room through the slats of the blinds pulled down against the fierce, noontime sun. The self-portrait of Vicki that had brought them together hung on the wall facing the large, leather-topped desk.

"Hello, Timothy." Vicki held her hand out to the corporation's executive vice-president, a portly man of Max's father's generation who had steered the twenty-five-year-old Max through his first years at the helm.

"How's Sally?" she asked, remembering that Timothy's wife had been unwell in the past few months.

"Much better, thanks. I can't understand why women have to have such complicated insides." He sighed.

"Oh, I was always taught it had something to do with the Garden of Eden." Vicki chuckled.

"Any chance of a kiss for your husband?" Max inquired

plaintively.

"I came to invite you for lunch," Vicki stated.

"You've been up to something." Max examined her closely with dancing eyes.

"No," she denied hastily. "What makes you say that?"

"You have that 'hand in the cookie jar' look about you." He grinned. "Come here and 'fess up."

Vicki laughed and came toward him. He brushed her lips lightly with his own, then stood back. "You've been closeted with Dan," he told her shrewdly.

"How do you know?" Vicki frowned, puzzled.

"Your hair smells of smoke."

Victoria sighed in acknowledgment. "It's inevitable, even after five minutes in his company. Shall I go splash myself with your cologne?"

Max chuckled. "No, I don't think so. It would create far too confusing a mixture!"

Timothy Hudson laughed. "If you'd grown up with a grandfather who was never seen without a fat Havana cigar between his lips, Vicki dear, you'd understand."

"Oh, I do," Vicki acquiesced. "I don't like it myself, but I'm just so used to it, now." She turned back to Max. "How about lunch, love? Or do you have other plans?"

"None that I can't change," he said easily.

Once the door had closed on Timothy's retreating back, Max pulled her toward him, kissing her with that firm, cool possession that, as always, left her breathless and quivering.

"You shouldn't do that," Vicki murmured, "unless you're prepared to follow through. It's not fair."

"There's always the couch!" Max took her face between his hands, his blue eyes turning purple again.

"I thought I was taking you out for lunch," Vicki said firmly, pulling away from his grasp.

Max laughed resignedly. "Such a single-minded creature! Where would you like to go?"

"I'm treating you, remember? You choose." Determinedly, she ducked the hand that snaked toward her, evidently intending to take hold of her strawberry-blond waves.

"In that case, it has to be the Oak Room," he said smoothly.

"Stinker!" Vicki grinned. "I suppose I asked for that one."

"You did! But don't worry, we'll split the check if your budget can't cover it."

Vicki gave a gurgle of laughter and perched herself on his desk as he punched the button for Lois. He asked the secretary to reserve a table and then looked across at Vicki, eyebrows quirked. "You want to walk or ride?"

"Ride," she declared unequivocally. "It's an oven out there."

"Ask Ed to bring the car around, would you, Lois?"

Once seated in the cool, dark atmosphere of the Oak Room, Max smiled across at his wife. She was, he decided, looking even more radiant than usual. There was an extra sparkle in those green eyes and a soft glow to the tanned complexion. She was excited about something, but he knew her well enough by now to realize that she would tell him in her own good time and not before.

He turned swiftly toward the waiter who appeared at his elbow. "Baked clams, Caesar salad, two broiled sole, and a bottle of the Pouligny Montrachet, please." The waiter nodded and disappeared as Vicki closed her menu with a resigned shrug.

"How did you know that's what I want to eat?"

"Tell me I was wrong," he challenged.

"You know you weren't. You always know. We've been together a bit less than two years and you behave as if you know everything about me!"

"Oh, not everything," he said seriously, "but I've made a good start."

Vicki shook her head in feigned despair, but kept silent as the wine appeared, followed rapidly by the clams.

"You are the most sensual woman, Victoria." Max speared a clam, his eyes alight with humor and something else—love, Vicki decided with a thrill of joy. "Watching you eat these is like watching you make love."

"I have a proposition to make." Vicki changed the subject firmly although her own eyes were responding to his.

"I knew there had to be a catch," Max groaned. "Why would such a beautiful, exciting woman invite me for lunch unless she had an ulterior motive?"

"Don't be absurd," Vicki said briskly, taking a slow, savoring sip of her wine. "Dan's discovered a new young sculptor. I don't know much about him, but his work is incredibly exciting. I saw two bronze statuettes this morning, and to put it bluntly, I have to have them. Apart from the fact that, unless I've really got it wrong, they're going to be a great investment, they're quite beautiful."

"Go on," Max prompted, dipping a piece of bread in the buttery sauce on his plate.

"Well," Vicki looked up from her own plate, "I could buy them myself, but it would clean me out until Dan processes the contracts I signed last week. That's going to take a couple of months and I don't want to wait that long."

"So, Victoria, what are you proposing? A loan, a partnership, or a gift?" Max asked calmly.

"Certainly not a gift," Vicki expostulated.

"Why not? Do you imagine I wouldn't give you whatever you asked?"

"I know damn well you would," she said firmly. "You're too generous for anybody's good. But if you think I'm going to ask you for ten thousand dollars, you can think again! The fact that you'd give it to me without even wanting to know why I want it is not the point."

"Here." Max held his last clam on his fork to her lips. "I'm incapable of denying you anything."

"Infatuated, are you? Totally besotted?" Vicki teased, taking the offering. Her green eyes were narrowed and glinting with promise and anticipation.

"Oh, I wouldn't put it quite that strongly," Max replied blandly. "But when you look at me like that, I lose all desire to go back to work this afternoon."

Oh, Lord, Victoria thought, as the familiar, liquid weakness spread through her. "Maybe we could just go back to the apartment?" she suggested thoughtfully.

"Victoria, you are a woman of immoderate appetites," Max informed her sternly. "Since you won't accept a gift, what's it to be—a loan or a partnership?"

Vicki pulled a face at him. "*You* got me off track, Max Randall. It's not my fault I can't look at you without wanting to love you."

"Get to the point, green eyes. Otherwise we'll both be in trouble!"

Vicki sighed. "Okay. I'd prefer a partnership, of course,

but you'd need to see the bronzes for yourself if you want to invest. If you'd rather make me a loan for a couple of months, I'd pay the usual interest."

"Are you suggesting I charge my wife interest on a loan?" he exclaimed.

Vicki saw the incredulous exasperation on his face and acknowledged that she had made a mistake. "Sorry. That was a little silly."

"A *little?*"

"All right, *very* silly," she conceded.

"Eat your lunch while I think about it." Max turned his attention to his sole, and for a while they ate in silence. Eventually, he looked up. "I can meet you at the gallery at five-thirty, if you're prepared to stay in town that long."

"Sure. I've got plenty to do," Vicki responded instantly. "You'll like them, Max."

"I know I will. I don't actually need to see them, my love. If you say they're good, that's enough for me." She placed a gentle hand over his, rubbing the hard knuckles, turning the palm over, running a thumb across its broad, lined flatness. "I want you to share them with me, love," Vicki said simply.

Max nodded in utter comprehension and called for the check. He gestured toward Vicki when the waiter came over and, with a quiet smile, she paid up.

"Well, what do you think?" Vicki looked at Max anxiously as he examined the smooth, cold, delicate pieces of bronze later that afternoon.

"You're the expert," he teased, knowing how she hated that expression.

"Come on, Max, otherwise I'll start yelling again," Vicki threatened.

"You do, my love, and we'll both regret it," he responded smoothly, taking one of the sculptures over to the light. Vicki followed him. Max never did anything in a hurry, she thought affectionately. He treated life in the way he was treating these sculptures, slowly savoring, working things out, making up his mind deliberately but decisively. She was much quicker, but none the less decisive.

"All right, wife, partners—in this as in everything." He held out his free hand and she clasped it strongly, expressing with her loving smile her absolute concurrence with his statement.

"Well, I'm glad you sorted that one out." Dan breezed in cheerfully. "I've been waiting to open the champagne, and the contracts are all ready for your signatures."

"One contract, one signature," Max announced briskly. "If you insist, Victoria, you can give me a check for your half later. It's silly to mess around with endless pieces of paper."

Vicki shrugged lightly. "Who's arguing?"

"You mean you're not?" He gazed at her in mock amazement.

"Go jump in the lake, Max." Grinning, she aimed a playful punch at his midriff. He caught her wrist easily, pulling her against him, bringing her arm around his waist.

"Good heavens!" Dan wiped his forehead expressively. "I think someone's tamed the shrew!"

"That, Dan, is the kind of chauvinistic remark I would expect from you, and it makes me very annoyed," Vicki retorted.

Dan grinned. "Why do you think I make them? I love to see you mad!"

"Well, I don't," Max stated firmly. "How about that champagne?"

Max let himself into the quiet house on a hot, sun-filled afternoon some days later and went through to the kitchen, where Josefa was ironing.

"Why, Mr. Max, what a surprise!" She smiled, putting down the iron. "Would you like lunch?"

"No thanks, Josefa. Where's Victoria?"

"Upstairs, in the bedroom, I think." She chuckled softly. "Judging by the thumps and bangs, I reckon she's rather busy."

"Doing what?" Max asked.

"Oh, I wouldn't know," the housekeeper replied, returning to her task with a quiet smile.

Max grinned. Josefa had been his grandfather's housekeeper, and he knew that it was only Victoria's easy, relaxed charm that had compensated Josefa for his wife's unorthodox behavior. Somehow, Victoria had managed to convince the housekeeper that, while she didn't want her to take over the household completely, she was still very much needed. What an extraordinary creature was his wife! Sometimes sophisticated, sometimes the most outrageous tomboy; elegant when she chose, but capable of the ultimate in scruffiness; but perpetually sensitive, warm, responsive to others, and always her own person. If only she would let him in on the darker side of herself—the side revealed only in her work. There was an aspect of Victoria that Max suspected no one knew, not even her brothers, and yet it was revealed in every one of her paintings.

Pausing in the bedroom doorway, he gazed in amazement at the chaos—the floor was covered in shoes! "Victoria, what on earth is going on?" For answer, an unaimed sandal flew through the room, landing at his feet. Max picked it up thoughtfully, a smile curving his lips as he crossed the room to the closet. He swung the sole of the sandal against the only visible part of his wife's anatomy, and she backed out of the closet with an indignant gasp.

"What was that for?" Vicki demanded, sitting back on her heels, looking up at him.

"Well, apart from the fact that it was utterly irresistible," he grinned, "it seemed the only way to get your attention. Just what are you doing?"

Vicki grimaced. "I was looking for a pair of shoes that I haven't been able to find for weeks, and things got kind of out of hand." She gestured around the room. "You wouldn't believe how dirty it is in here."

"Oh, but I would! Most of the dirt has been transferred to you. You've got dust balls in your hair and cobwebs hanging from your eyebrows!"

"Am I too dirty to kiss?" Vicki raised her eyebrows quizzically, still sitting on her heels. His eyes were alight with that curious mixture of desire and amusement that never failed to fill her with love and the absolute sense of being loved.

"I think I'd rather give you a bath first." The gravity of his tone was belied by his languorous, anticipatory expression.

"I don't think that would be a very good idea," she bantered, denying the weakness that flooded her body at the prospect.

"And why not?" His eyes narrowed, but he made no move to touch her. The sexually charged atmosphere crackled between them as they waited, putting off the inevitable physical contact and enjoying the waiting.

"Well, I'd never get this mess cleared up, would I?" Vicki responded prosaically, her gaze never leaving his.

Max scratched his head, a thoughtful frown on his face as he considered her. "I'm sure this is a stupid question, and that the answer is quite simple, but I have to ask it anyway." He paused for a second.

"Get to the point," Vicki demanded.

"Just why, when we have a full-time housekeeper who is ably assisted by an almost full-time maid, are you cleaning out your own closet?" Max planted his hands firmly on his hips as he spoke.

"Ahh . . ." Vicki responded, equally thoughtfully. "To tell the truth, I don't like people interfering in my—"

"Space?" he finished, a quizzical lift to his eyebrows.

"If you like." She shrugged. "But, actually, I'd be rather ashamed to have anyone else deal with this chaos."

"I knew there had to be a simple answer." He chuckled softly.

"Now, perhaps you'll tell me what you're doing home at this time of the day." Vicki examined one of the discarded shoes critically, pulling at a loose strap.

"I was planning a little love-in-the-afternoon," Max murmured. "I hadn't expected to find you on your hands and knees in the closet, covered in dust!"

"I'm not entirely sure I believe you, Max. There has to be another reason." She laughed up at him, noting the slight, conscious flash in his eyes.

"I have a couple of calls to make. I can give you five minutes to get this mess cleaned up and yourself in an upright position. Then I'll tell you," he said briskly.

"Five minutes, huh?" Vicki considered him. "That's your best offer?"

"It is." He was still standing over her, feet apart, hands on hips. The embodiment of masculinity, Vicki thought distractedly. There was such contained power in those long, powerful legs, the slim hips, broad chest, and wide shoulders, so much love and sensitivity in that rugged face, in those blue eyes that could so readily soften with compassion or desire.

"Oh, well." She shrugged cheerfully. "I wasn't exactly having fun, anyway." She began to toss the shoes back into the closet in a random, haphazard fashion, Max's laugh ringing in her ears as he went downstairs.

Some minutes later, when the shower door slid open, Vicki was standing, eyes tight shut under the cascade of water, massaging shampoo vigorously into her scalp. "Who's that?" She put her head back under the spray.

"Who were you expecting?" came the light, swift response.

"You'll get water all over the floor," she grumbled, ignoring his question.

"So?"

Vicki reached for the conditioner, eyes still tight shut, squeezing some into the palm of her hand. "Are you coming in, too, or do you fancy the voyeur role?" She grinned blindly.

"The latter at the moment." The soft, suggestive voice

stroked over her body, bringing prickly tingles to life across her wet skin. It was the oddest sensation, Vicki thought, being watched when one's eyes were shut.

"I'm thinking of all the wonderful things I'm going to do with you, if you ever decide to get out." The sensual throb in his voice made her catch her breath. This bantering antic- ipation was so much an integral part of their lovemaking.

"You still haven't told me why, apart from the obvious, you're home in the middle of the afternoon." Vicki deliber- ately made her tone prosaic to prolong the waiting.

"I have to go to Los Angeles rather unexpectedly this evening."

"Oh." She stood on one leg, soaping her foot. "I'll miss you."

"You could always come, too." It was both invitation and statement, but for the moment she missed the invitation.

"No thanks, it'll give me a chance to do some work," she said easily, rinsing off the conditioner with firm fingers. As the shower door clicked quietly shut, the cold realization of how Max would interpret her remark crept over her.

The door slammed back on its runners, shaking the fabric of its construction as she catapulted, wet and dripping, across the bathroom and into the bedroom. Max, with his usual methodical efficiency, was putting clothes into a small suitcase on the bed.

"Darling, I didn't mean that as it sounded!" She grabbed his arms, pulling him around to face her. "I didn't mean that I can't work when you're here, it's just that . . ."

"Just that what, Victoria?" Such cold hurt in his eyes and in his voice; how could she ever get through to him?

"Once in a while I have to be alone, particularly when

84

I'm blocked as I am now. I need to be able to work without thinking of anyone else; eating and sleeping when and if I want to. It's the way I work, Max; please try to understand . . ." Her voice faded under his frozen expression.

"I thought I *was* trying, Victoria. I do my best not to encroach on your 'space.'" The heavy emphasis he placed on the last word hung in the air between them and she stood silent, heedless of the water running off her body, making small puddles on the oak floor.

Max gently removed her hands from his arms before going into the bathroom. "Here." He wrapped a thick bath towel around her. "Bend your head." As she obeyed, frustrated misery overwhelming her, he rubbed the clinging water out of her hair with a second towel. "Listen to me, my love." His hands continued to work through her hair. "You told me many times before you eventually agreed to marry me that you weren't the marrying kind. I took a gamble by continuing to press you, but you did agree voluntarily. We have a lot to learn about compromise and a lot to learn about each other. I'm sorry I reacted quite so quickly just now—I suppose I'm more needy than you are, but you're going to have to compact that space a little, if we're going to make a go of this."

As he lifted the towel from her head, Vicki looked up at him gravely. "I'm willing to try to compact the space, but you have to be willing to accept that my need to be alone is *not* a rejection of you. It's a positive necessity. I have a job to do, Max, and on occasion time to myself is a prerequisite."

"I don't see how I'm denying that." Max shook his head helplessly, his eyes asking for explanation and understanding.

She was unable to give them to him. "As you say, we've a long way to go." With a slight shrug, Vicki moved away, giving up the attempt to get him to understand, and wrapped the towel sarong-style under her arms. A year's entrancing courtship and nine months of idyllic marriage had clearly run up against a fairly large rock. But perhaps that was only to be expected—one couldn't live on cloud nine forever, and they were moving into a new phase; she just wasn't quite sure what tactics were appropriate for this stage.

"Damn you, Victoria!" Max exploded suddenly, surprisingly. "Let me show you what I mean by compromise! Take that towel off and get on the bed."

"I can't." Vicki stood her ground. "Your suitcase is in the way."

A Carrolton, of course, would have hurled the case and its contents to the floor, she thought with a detached part of her mind, watching Max remove it with one controlled, tidy movement. A hand grasped the towel between her breasts, stripping it off her body; a hard, flat palm pushed her backward onto the bed. Vicki lay still, not frightened in the least by this unusual display, but rather curious and interested as she watched him throw off his clothes with unusual carelessness.

"Is this Carrolton or Randall anger?" Vicki inquired as, naked, he towered over her.

"Let's hope it's Carrolton! Good Lord, what *am* I doing?" Realization struck him and a look of amazement crossed his face, chasing away the darkness. And then they were both laughing. Vicki pulled him down on the bed beside her, rolling on top of him, digging her knees into the mattress as she straddled his supine body, her fingers curled in the soft hairs of his chest.

"Truce?" She grinned, invoking the surrender word of her childhood.

Max seized her hips, fingers digging into the firm muscles as he lifted her, guiding her body to receive him. Holding her strongly, he smiled up into her face and inquired, "Truce, Victoria?"

"Perhaps not," she whispered. "I think we have to play this one through to the end." Her hands slid along his body, until they rested on his shoulders, pinioning them to the mattress. Circling her hips slowly, rhythmically, she felt him move inside her and laughed in soft delight. "Fast or slow, Max? I'm in charge."

"Only for as long as I allow you to be," he countered with a mischievous smile. His hands grasped one breast, squeezing gently, drawing it into his mouth as she hung above him. Vicki moaned softly, all the turmoil of the last minutes banished as they joined in love and he moved his body upward, matching his rhythm to her own. The sun pouring in through the open window was hot on her back. His hands moved down her spine to cup her buttocks as their shared passion peaked.

Holding her firmly against him, Max raised his body to meet her at the arc of her fulfillment. With a long, deep sigh, she fell against his chest, her heart pounding against his as they lay bathed in sunlight, their fusion, for this time anyway, overcoming the conflict.

"You're a wicked woman, Victoria," Max groaned eventually, rolling her off him. "How could you make me behave like that?"

"Oh, I thought it was fun," Vicki murmured innocently. "I'm sorry you didn't enjoy it."

"You know damn well what I mean!" His fingers twisted in her still-wet hair, holding her head tightly as his eyes glowed with amusement and the residue of passion. "Just for that, you can drive me to the airport."

"I was going to, anyway," Vicki announced in dignified accents.

That night she lay wide-eyed and sleepless, alone in the large bed in the silent house, staring into the darkness. It was ridiculous; but she felt so lonely! Watching Max disappear into the departure lounge, her lips carrying the impression of his fierce kiss, she had felt curiously bereft. In the last twenty-one months they had spent a few nights apart, but not many since they had been married. Perhaps she was losing her capacity to be alone. Slowly, the thought began to crystallize and excitement surged through her. Loneliness— that was what she had been trying to express in the third painting of the holocaust series, but she hadn't recognized it. She hadn't really experienced the emotion before—her own company had always been too precious. With a swift movement, Vicki flicked the light switch and got energetically out of bed. After a quick shower, she pulled on a pair of faded jeans and a paint-stained but clean shirt. In the kitchen, she piled apples, cheese, milk, and coffee on a tray, as if preparing for a siege, before disappearing into the studio, shutting the door firmly on the outside world.

There was no phone in the room—she had reacted with undisguised horror to Max's suggestion that they put one in. Josefa came up several times a day with trays of food, but otherwise left her alone. Occasionally, usually in the middle of the night, Vicki would drift down to the kitchen to make herself a sandwich. She was oblivious to time as the image of a lonely, devastated world after the ultimate horror took shape under her brush.

Four days later, at six o'clock in the morning, Max stood motionless in the doorway of the studio. Victoria lay asleep, barefoot but fully dressed, on the patchwork cover of the old sofa that had been in every studio she had ever used. He picked up the half-empty mug of coffee on the table—it was tepid. Obviously, she had been working all night.

The painting screamed its message at him, and he stood for a long time allowing it to seep through his pores, to chill the very marrow in his bones. How could this bright, laughing, sensual, mischievous, infuriating creature of the sun produce such an image of horror and desolation?

"What do you think?"

Her quiet voice broke the silence, and he turned, going over to the couch. "I can see why you need your space," he said softly, dropping to his haunches beside her, running one hand through her wavy hair, his eyes exploring the deep purple shadows on the drained yet peaceful face.

"You're exhausted," he said gently.

"Mmm." Vicki nodded slightly.

"Come along. I'm going to give you a bath and put you to bed." He slid his hands under her body, lifting her up as he rose to his feet.

"Playing Svengali to my Trilby again, Max?" Vicki questioned, a hint of the old impish grin in her tired eyes.

"Do you mind?" Max held her, prepared to accept the answer, whatever it might be.

"No. It's rather nice, actually. Now that I'm all through, that is. It wouldn't have been before." Her eyes were serious as she looked to see if he understood what she was saying.

"From now on I'll try to arrange my business trips to fit in with your creative needs." Max smiled suddenly. "But four days is quite long enough. You don't look as if you've washed your face since I left!"

"I probably haven't. I can't really remember."

In their bedroom, he placed her gently on the bed before filling the tub with hot water and a few drops of scented bath oil.

"I'm quite capable of doing this myself," Vicki protested mildly as he began to undress her.

"I know you are, but I'm enjoying myself—okay?" He pulled off her jeans with one swift movement, lifting her body easily as he did so.

"Okay," Vicki concurred. "So am I, actually."

"I know you are," Max repeated, looking at the rosy nipples standing out against the small, pointed breasts. Vicki laughed softly, yielding her body to his ministrations. In this state of satisfied exhaustion, it was delicious to lie still and passive under those strong hands as they soaped her with gentle thoroughness, turning her body, lifting her, drying her, before depositing her firmly in the bed.

"Aren't you coming in, too?" Vicki invited as he tucked her in tightly, smoothing the sheet.

"Not right now. I've got some calls to make first. Get some sleep, little love. When I do come, I'll expect you to be ready for me!" Max laughed at her disappointed expression, kissing her forehead lightly before closing the door gently on his already unconscious wife.

Vicki hurtled down the stairs from the studio, grabbing up the telephone in the hallway, desperate to silence its shrill, impatient demands. "Hello?" she gasped breathlessly.

"Where the hell have you been? I've been calling nonstop for the last hour!"

She gazed in disbelief at the inanimate receiver. The barely suppressed rage rasping over the wire was something she had never heard from Max before.

"In the studio," she explained, bewildered.

"Well, why didn't Josefa answer the phone?"

"I gave her the day off. What's the . . .?"

"Dammit, Victoria, we're going to have to do something about this when I get back! It's utterly ridiculous that I can't get hold of you in an emergency!"

"Get back from where? What emergency?" Completely at sea now, Vicki slid down the wall, dropping cross-legged onto the pale olive carpet.

"I'm leaving for Quebec immediately. I don't know how long I'll be away."

"But why? What's happened? Aren't you coming home first?" The questions tumbled over themselves in her confusion.

"I haven't time to explain now. If you'd answered the phone when I first called, I'd have been able to."

"I'm sorry," she said helplessly.

"Yes—well, it's not going to happen again, I can promise you that. I don't need this sort of aggravation! I'll try and call you tomorrow evening—I won't have time before then."

"Take care then, darling." There wasn't much else to say in the circumstances.

"You, too." A slight note of warmth crept into his voice. "I have to run, love. Ed's here with the car. Talk to you later."

Vicki replaced the silent receiver, a puzzled frown marring her smooth features. What on earth was going on? She suddenly realized that she didn't even know where he was staying in Quebec. Thoughtfully, she dialed the office number—Lois would have that information.

"Mr. Randall's office," the secretary's crisp voice answered on the third ring.

"Hi, Lois, it's Vicki."

"Oh, Mrs. Randall, I'm so sorry about all that," Lois said sympathetically.

"You heard, eh?" Vicki grinned slightly in spite of herself.

"I've never seen him like this—he's acting just like his grandfather. Why, he even shouted at me." This last piece of information was imparted in tones of total incredulity.

"Oh, poor Lois! At least I was at the other end of the telephone. What's happened?"

"I just don't know, Mrs. Randall. There was a conference call on his private line, and then he was demanding an instant reservation on the next flight. He's in a towering rage." Lois's voice dropped and Vicki thought she could detect tears in the slight sniff that followed.

"Listen, Lois," she said briskly. "Whatever it is, it has nothing to do with you—or me, for that matter. Can you imagine how penitent he's going to be when he cools off?"

A watery chuckle came out of the receiver. "That's

better," Vicki stated firmly. "Now, can you give me the details of his hotel and get me a seat on the earliest available flight? Oh, and Lois, book it tourist, please." It was necessary to tell the secretary that. Vicki smiled to herself. Lois had probably never booked an economy-class ticket in all her years at the Randall Corporation!

"Tourist!" Lois's horror rang in Vicki's ears. "Mr. Randall would insist you travel first class."

"I don't see him anywhere, do you?" Vicki chuckled, "Charge it to my American Express, would you? I'll give you the number."

"But surely it should go on the company's travel account?" Lois sounded even more alarmed.

Vicki sighed. She'd only asked Lois to do this for her to take the other woman's mind off her shock. Clearly, it had not been a good idea. "This is not a company expense, Lois," she told her firmly. "Neither is it Max's expense. I can assure you that if he screams at anyone, it'll be me." Not that he would, she thought fondly. He'd give an exasperated shake of the head, maybe, but nothing more.

She was throwing clothes into two suitcases when the phone rang again. "There's a flight to Montreal at two o'clock this afternoon, Mrs. Randall, with a connection to Quebec that you should make if everything goes according to plan."

"That's great, Lois," Vicki answered enthusiastically. "If I miss the connection, which I won't," she added confidently, "I'll simply have to stay overnight in Montreal. Just give me the details."

Lois sounded much more cheerful as she relayed flight numbers and times with her usual brisk competence, and

Vicki began to feel the familiar, exciting adrenaline pump as she contemplated this impulsive flight into the unknown. But it wasn't quite like the unknowns of her past—Max would be at the end of this journey.

She spent a swift twenty minutes briefing Josefa, calling a cab, shutting up her studio—as usual, turning everything away from the door—before diving under the shower. She rejected the nostalgic inclination to backpack in a pair of jeans in favor of a soft suede skirt and jacket whose understated elegance declared both its fairly astronomical price and Max's taste, and made the flight by the skin of her crocodile shoes.

Miraculously, as sometimes happened, everything went according to plan and she arrived at Le Château Frontenac in Quebec just as the sun began to dip over the St. Lawrence. The river gleamed below the castlelike structure of the hilltop hotel, which dominated the walled city with its turrets and towers. The lobby was fairly chaotic, the reception desk thronged with guests and potential guests, questioning, demanding—some aggressive, some resigned, some quietly polite.

Vicki took her place in line, keeping half an eye on the suitcases placed by the doorman just inside the doors. When she eventually reached the desk, she spoke to the clerk in French, mainly out of courtesy but just a little because it would facilitate her exchange. She didn't speak the dialect and could not pretend that she was a French-Canadian, but she could pass for native French under the most relentless linguistic scrutiny . . . and when you wanted a favor in Quebec, it did you no harm!

All the same, she had some trouble convincing the desk

clerk that it was quite legitimate for her to achieve entrance to Mr. Randall's room without his authorization. However, after several identifying documents, a couple of laughing innuendoes about surprising one's husband, and many warm smiles, she was escorted to the large, comfortable room overlooking the river. She was given her own key; the clerk held on to Max's and promised that he would not divulge to Mr. Randall that another key had been issued.

The door shut on the departing bellman, and Vicki prowled around a room that showed no signs of occupancy. Closets and drawers were empty, but that was not surprising since, as far as she knew, Max had left without luggage. One of her two suitcases contained his clothes. Vicki had laughed at herself as she packed them. It was such a wifely, protective thing to do, and probably totally unnecessary since Max was quite capable of buying what he needed on the spot. But some instinct had told her that he was in trouble, and she had been no more able to prevent herself from packing a few of his things than she had been to resist the impulse to join him.

The bathroom revealed a small, complimentary airline pack of toiletries, clearly used, judging by the wet bristles of the tiny traveling toothbrush. Vicki turned on the faucets in the tub and wandered back into the bedroom, stripping off her clothes thoughtfully, dropping them carelessly where they fell. She had no idea when Max would return—he was presumably still at the Quebec office, unless he had gone out for dinner. But that was unlikely; it was still early, and they both preferred to eat later in the evening. Well, she'd find out soon enough. She stepped into the tub with a sigh of plea-sure as the hot water eased her travel-weary body.

"What brings you here?" Max stood in the bathroom doorway, his quiet question jerking her out of the half-sleep partly induced by the soothing water and partly self-induced in preparation for whatever the rest of the day might hold.

"You," Vicki responded, equally quietly. There was no welcome on the drawn, haggard, gray-complexioned face, and uncharacteristic uncertainty suddenly overpowered her. "I hope I haven't disrupted any plans?" she said, unable to keep the slight, nervous smile off her face.

"If by that you mean was I expecting to find another naked lady in my tub, the answer is no." He turned back into the bedroom and Vicki shivered, aware now of the rapidly cooling bath water. She hadn't really meant that, but, if she had, in normal circumstances it would have provided the opportunity for playful retribution, not this cold withdrawal. She struggled to identify the look on Max's face, rubbing herself dry vigorously with the large bath towel. Then it came to her—defenseless. That strong, assertive, never-fazed husband of hers looked as if he'd been kicked repeatedly in the stomach and had collapsed, beaten and undefended, under the attack. She pulled on a terry-cloth robe, tying the belt unnecessarily tight, recognizing with a detached part of her brain that this was no time for provocative clothing. The soft, vulnerable part of her had to be kept well wrapped.

"Do you want a drink?" Max turned from the window as she came through into the room.

"Please," Vicki responded, watching him as he opened the mini-bar, trying to find a clue in his bearing to tell her what she should do next.

"Campari?"

"Yes, thank you." She took the glass and Max turned back to the window, a strange, unnerving sag to his broad shoulders. "Max . . ." she began slowly, taking a sip of her drink.

He spun around. "I don't want you here, Victoria. I have enough to think about as it is."

Harsh pain filled her and she turned her back, fighting the hurt, knowing somehow that it wasn't intentional. This must be how Max had felt when she had excluded him from areas of her life with her demand for space. "I'll leave in the morning," Vicki said quietly, amazed at the steadiness of her voice. "I'm sure I could get another room for tonight, if you'd rather I went now."

The silence stretched into an infinity of pain. They didn't know each other after all—they were just two separate beings who had decided to join forces. There was nothing she could offer him at this crisis point in his life that he was prepared to accept.

"Why don't you just unpack, Victoria?" Max broke the silence wearily, bending to pick up her discarded clothing.

"I'll do that." She moved swiftly toward him.

"Damn right you will!" He dumped the clothes into her arms. "This room was immaculate—now look at it!" He gestured with an outflung, impatient arm at the opened suitcase and tumbled contents.

"I'd said I'd leave," Vicki heard herself snap, furious with herself for losing patience but unable to prevent it.

Max looked at her and felt some of the tension leave his body—she was so little, he thought distractedly, yet so full of life, love, and strength—a strength that she was freely offering and that he was rejecting.

"You're not going anywhere. I need you." The words

reached her on a rasping sob, and with a deep sigh Vicki slipped her arms around him, offering the strength that at last he received.

"Tell me about it, love." She eased him across the room, pulling his unresisting body down onto the bed beside her, cradling his head against her breast.

"It's hard to tell."

Vicki waited quietly, one hand tenderly stroking back the black hair from the broad forehead.

"Gilles has been embezzling for the last five years. We missed it, Victoria! An entire staff of accountants, auditors, and whatnot missed it! And *I* missed it." The voice dropped to a low, defeated whisper. "Gilles was one of my closest friends." The flat statement ended the explanation, and Vicki sat silently, absorbing Max's pain. For someone with his integrity, his powerful loyalty and honesty, the betrayal of a friend, someone whom he had trusted implicitly, would be the ultimate treachery.

"Who's here with you, love?" she asked, keeping her voice calm, matter-of-fact.

"Timothy, Jack Greyson, our New York accountant, and all the chief accountants and auditors in the Quebec office."

"How about the police?"

"They've been notified, but we have to find out the full extent of the embezzlement first, and exactly how he did it, before I turn it over completely."

"How did it come out?"

"A slight discrepancy, picked up by a bright young auditor—he dug a little deeper." Max shrugged. "I cannot *believe* I was so blind! All these years, Victoria! I would have trusted Gilles with anything."

"Let's ease up on the emotional side of this for a while." She pulled herself up against the headboard, still holding him tightly against her. "How serious is it, financially?"

"That, my love, is what I'm here to find out." Max sat up, and for the first time in twelve hours a smile glinted in his eyes. "You don't need to cuddle me anymore, Mama, I'm all better now."

"I can still cuddle you." Vicki smiled softly.

"Sure you can. But right now I have to shower and get back to the office. I only came back to grab a sandwich." He began to undress swiftly.

"Well, I'm sorry a naked lady in your tub held you up," she teased, beginning to get dressed. "I brought you some clothes—they're in the other suitcase."

"Bless you, wife." He squeezed her shoulders as he passed. "I haven't had a chance to buy a change of under-clothes!"

"I'm glad I'm here." Vicki followed him into the bath-room. "I wouldn't have enjoyed another telephone call like this morning's."

"Oh, yes, now that's another thing." Max squeezed tooth-paste on his brush.

"Let's discuss it later," Vicki said lightly, sitting on the edge of the tub to pull on her socks.

"Nothing to discuss, green eyes! This is a non-negotiable statement. A telephone with a private line goes into that studio of yours as soon as we get home." He stepped under the shower, and the rush of water drowned out her response.

Vicki pulled back the curtain, stating firmly, "On one con-dition."

"I said it was non-negotiable. What's the matter with your

hearing?" A sodden washcloth flew through the air. Vicki ducked just in time, picked it up, and hurled it back.

"One condition," she reiterated. "You don't call me up to ask what's for dinner."

"Agreed. Not that you'd know anyway, once you're immersed." Max stepped out of the shower. "Pass me a towel." His fingers snapped imperatively, and with a grin, Vicki tossed him one, resisting the urge to use it herself on his long, masculine body—this was clearly not a time for play. She wandered back into the bedroom, searching through her still-unpacked suitcase.

Max followed rapidly and peered into the closet. "We're going to have a problem with hangers. Call housekeeping and ask them to send some up, will you?"

"It didn't take you long to recover your bossiness, did it?" Vicki mumbled through the neck of her sweater, pulling it over her head.

"Don't provoke me, Victoria. I haven't the time to react!" Max laughed. "You'd better have this room cleared up by the time I get back."

"I'm coming with you," she declared flatly. "And that, Max Randall, is non-negotiable!"

"In that case," he said, pulling up the zipper of his cord pants, "I'll call for the hangers while you get on with the unpacking. By the time we get back, we'll be too exhausted to do anything."

"How disappointing," she murmured, obediently attacking her clothes.

"I can't imagine how I ever got myself married to a speed demon and a sex maniac!" Max heaved an exaggerated sigh and picked up the bedside phone. "I'll get room service to send up a couple of club sandwiches—will that do you?"

"It may not be the Tour d'Argent, but I'll survive." Vicki chuckled.

The group waiting for them in the large board room was a disheveled, fatigued, sad-looking one, Vicki thought as Max introduced her quickly.

Timothy Hudson kissed her lightly, his eyes heavy with strain and weariness. "I'm glad you're here, Vicki," he said quietly. "This is really tough on Max."

"Yes, I know." She smiled her understanding and turned to shake hands with Jack Greyson.

"Okay, let's get started." Max pushed a pile of ledgers across the table, toward Vicki. "We don't know what we're looking for, Victoria. Gilles seems to have used a variety of systems; we've discovered three so far and God only knows how many more there are! They're all very clever. It's a bit like cracking a code—you look for a pattern, however unlikely it seems, and then work through it, trying to find a combination—okay?"

"I guess so." She shrugged. "It sounds a lot like looking for the proverbial needle in the haystack."

"It is." Max gave a slight, twisted grin. They were all speaking English in deference to Jack, whose French was of the schoolboy variety at best, but for the next half-hour the only sounds were those of pages turning.

"Is Gilles giving absolutely no help on this?" Vicki asked in sudden exasperation. "I mean, he knows the game's up, what's he got to lose, for heaven's sake?"

"He's playing cat and mouse with us," Max informed her quietly. "It's almost as if he's challenging us to find it all out."

Vicki used a French expletive that caused a quick gasp to run around the table.

"Where on earth did you learn that?" Max exclaimed.

"From a sailor in Marseilles," she replied cheerfully.

Max sighed. "Silly question—I can't imagine why I asked."

"Sorry." She looked up with a quick grin. "It just slipped out—seemed appropriate, somehow."

"Utterly appropriate, Madame Randall," an elegant, gray-haired Canadian concurred with grave courtesy. "You said it for us all."

Silence reigned again, and after what seemed an eternity, Vicki sighed, pressing her hands into the small of her back, easing the stiff muscles.

"Let's get you a cab, Victoria." Max pushed back his chair. "It's eleven o'clock."

"No, I'm fine," she said swiftly. "I wouldn't mind some coffee, though."

"There's a machine down the hall," someone offered.

"Let's take a break then," Max said firmly. "We'll all be the better for it."

It was over an hour later when Vicki looked again at the pad at her elbow, in a room where the only sounds were the crackle of paper, the soft tap of fingers punching calculators, and the slight, resigned thud of discarded, unyielding ledgers. The notations she'd jotted down made some kind of sense. It was a bizarre pattern, going back over four years, but if you could think divergently, it *did* make a pattern. She went back over the relevant pages—she was reluctant to say anything to this group of experts until she was as sure as she could be.

"I think there's something a little strange here," she said eventually. The instant attention her remark achieved was somewhat intimidating.

"Spit it out, love," Max said quietly.

"Well, I know it sounds silly . . ."

"Victoria, we're all playing in the dark—anything that seems to make a pattern for anyone here is enough to throw out for general consumption."

"Okay, then—it's not numbers but colors," Vicki stated definitely. "I work with colors, so maybe I'm seeing something that isn't there . . ."

"Madame Randall, Gilles is a very clever man," a soft voice interrupted her hesitant beginning. "If you, with your particular expertise, can see something that we can't, it may be very valuable."

"There's a pattern over the last four years. All the primary colors are used in rotation to write in a certain figure on the balance sheet—one hundred thousand dollars. It's written in either red, blue, or yellow, in that order, carefully spaced over the months and interspersed with many colored inks, so if you weren't looking for the organized pattern, you wouldn't notice."

"Show us, Victoria." Max stretched a long arm for the ledgers at her elbow. She flipped through them rapidly.

"Okay, but you're going to have to come around here," she said.

They all moved as one body to stand behind her, peering over her shoulder at the ledgers as she went through them.

"It's crazy," Max said after a long while, "but it's so damn crazy that it makes sense."

"It could just be a coincidence." Vicki shrugged, closing the last ledger.

"Yes, but unlikely, *madame*," the Canadian accountant said with sudden conviction. "It is very much the sort of scheme that would appeal to Gilles. He has a devious imagination."

"Very," Max muttered, an unconcealed bitterness underlying the curt agreement.

Vicki reached behind her for his hand, squeezed it comfortingly, and was reassured by the answering pressure.

"Let's call it a night," Max said briskly. "We'll see what the auditors can do with this possibility tomorrow. Come along, Victoria, say good night now—it's past your bedtime."

A slight smile ran over the weary faces of the men in the room at this firm, husbandly injunction. Vicki shot Max an exasperated glance and was rewarded with a mischievous wink that drew from her an involuntary chuckle as he bore her inexorably out into the night.

Total weariness overtook her on the cab ride back to their hotel—it had been an utterly draining day, emotionally more than physically; but then, that was always the worst. Once in their room, she sank with a heavy sigh onto the bed, only to be pulled firmly to her feet.

"You lie down now, my love, and you'll be asleep in your clothes. Brush your teeth and then I'll undress you." Max steered her into the bathroom, where he squeezed toothpaste on her brush, turned on the faucet, and stood over her as she completed her preparations.

"Max, I am quite capable of putting myself to bed," Vicki declared, her chuckle of protest lost in a deep, involuntary yawn.

"Oh, you are, are you?" He pulled her sweater over her head and proceeded to undress her with deft fingers. In seconds, it seemed, she had been rolled under the covers on the wide bed and firmly tucked in. Just before the bliss of unconsciousness captured her, Vicki registered Max's orderly movements as he put her clothes away in the closet.

❦ 8 ❦

Vicki awoke only because of a curiously empty, cold space on her stomach. Max's hand had left her body after a nighttime of possession. The sound of water running in the bathroom and then a brisk rap on the door brought her to dazed semiconsciousness. Someone wanted access, and since Max was under the shower, she would have to provide it. With a heavy groan, Vicki swung her legs out of the bed. Her fumbling fingers were wrestling ineffectually with the lock on the door when she realized she was naked.

"Get back into bed, green eyes." Max's amused voice, his hands on her shoulders, completed the waking-up process, and, sped by a friendly pat on the behind, she dived back under the covers. She watched surreptitiously as Max opened the door to admit a chambermaid with a steaming, laden tray.

The cheerful, joking exchange as he took the tray and signed the slip brought a slight, impish smile to Vicki's lips. "Such a pretty girl," she murmured. "Is that why you like to stay here?"

"Such an inquisitive wife!" Blue eyes sparkling, he brought a cup of coffee over to the bed.

"And aren't wives entitled to be curious?" Vicki demanded, hitching herself onto one elbow, taking the proffered cup.

"That rather depends," he teased, "on the area of curiosity."

"Max Randall, how dare you!" The coffee slurped dangerously close to the rim of the cup. "Are you implying that you might consider an . . . an affair?"

"And what would you say if I were?" He took the cup from her hand and placed it carefully on the night table.

Vicki regarded him through narrowed eyes, contemplating her response. "I would take measures to ensure your permanent inability to indulge." She grinned at him, opting for a joking response to a question that she knew she should not take seriously, but unable, then, to resist the soft, "What would you say if *I* were?"

"I intend to keep you so utterly satisfied, my love, that you'll have neither the energy nor the inclination for wandering," Max stated tranquilly, tossing his robe to the floor.

"It's six o'clock in the morning, after a very short night." Her murmured, feigned grumble fell on deaf ears as her husband, with a broad smile, dived onto the bed beside her, rolling her, with ruthless hands, beneath him. With a deep, relaxed sigh, Vicki spread herself to receive the taut, desiring body. Her hands, fingers splayed, moved down his back, grasping the tight, muscular buttocks as they moved him with rhythmic slowness in the warm, moist cave of her self.

"How I love it when you're all sleepy and relaxed like this," Max murmured against her ear, nipping the tender lobe between gentle teeth. "You smell of sleep and desire, and all you can do is lie here and let me take us both. Where would you like to go this morning, little love?"

"To a cradle in the treetops, rocked by a gentle breeze," she responded promptly.

"Don't move then, my own love. I'm on the edge and need no stimulation." He laughed softly. With willing compliance Vicki lay still, eyes locked with his as he held himself in check until he could tell by the sudden glow in the slanty eyes, the quick movement of tongue across mobile lips, that his wife had almost reached her treetop cradle.

Vicki moaned in soft delight as the gentle sweetness spread so very, very slowly through her belly, taking over her body as Max played her, as only he knew how, drawing the high notes of perfection from her to shatter in brilliant shards of light in the air above as they clung together in the treetops before tumbling in slow motion to the mossy ground beneath—in perfect peace and harmony.

Vicki's eyes closed again as her husband, her love, gently withdrew from her and she lay, naked, spread-eagled, and suffused with satisfaction on the bed. Max covered her with the sheet and brushed her forehead with tender lips before getting reluctantly to his feet.

"Get some sleep, now, green eyes. I'll put the DO NOT DISTURB card on the door." Seeing her still and unresponsive, a smile quivered on his lips and he bent over her again. "Victoria, can you hear me?"

"Mmm."

"Reserve us a table—anywhere you like—for dinner tonight. I'll be back by seven o'clock—all right?"

"Was going to come with you," the drowsy voice murmured.

"Just be well rested by tonight, my sweet." Max chuckled and continued his dressing, satisfied that the small, curled mound under the covers was far gone in sleep. He closed the door quietly behind him and left, with considerably more heart for his grim task than he had had yesterday.

Noon! It couldn't be! Vicki gazed in befuddled disbelief at her small gold wristwatch. Her memories of the earlier part of the morning were vague, to say the least, but surely Max had left before seven o'clock? If that were the case, she'd slept for another five hours. She gave a long, lazy, all-body stretch, and a general sense of well-being filled her. Only coffee was needed to ensure total contentment. After that, a shower and a leisurely jaunt about the town—it was a pleasing program.

She spent a blissful afternoon strolling around the walled town of old Quebec under a soft September sun. It was not a city she knew well, and she followed her feet and her inclination from the Place d'Armes, dominated by the castlelike structure of Le Château Frontenac, to Dufferin Terrace and the Champlain Monument standing way above the magnificent sweep of the St. Lawrence. From there she took the oldest elevator in North America down to Lower Town, wandering through streets redolent with history and the blood of many battles. It was a city with a strong European flavor, and Vicki was transported back to the exciting, freewheeling years of her struggles to find and develop Vicki Carrolton, to test, hone, and professionalize a talent that she had previously only recognized as a burning, all-consuming need to create.

She returned to the hotel at six o'clock, healthily tired,

spiritually renewed, to open a small bottle of champagne from the mini-bar and sink with a sigh of utter pleasure into a neck-high tub of very hot water.

Max walked into the room to be met by his fresh, sparkling wife in a simple sea-green cotton shift with white-edged capped sleeves that accentuated the peach-bloom of her slender arms and the deep-green lynx eyes that were dancing in the way that made him forget all else but his love and desire.

"Oh, my poor love. You look *so* tired," Vicki said compassionately. She hugged him briefly, then pushed off his jacket and loosened his tie. "Was it a horrible day?"

"It's improving rapidly." He smiled, willingly passive under her hands as she unbuttoned his shirt with serious concentration, lower lip caught between her teeth, a slight frown between the fine-drawn eyebrows.

"We don't have to go out tonight." Vicki pushed him gently onto the bed and bent to take off his shoes. "Room service and an early bedtime is fine by me."

"Not by me. I want the finest dinner that this gastronomic city has to offer." Max stood up to unfasten his belt and then chuckled as she pushed his hands away impatiently.

"Just keep still, husband. You did this for me last night— it's my turn now to play nurturer."

"You've been nurturing me ever since you arrived," he said softly, running his fingers through her bright red-gold hair. "In fact, ever since I met you."

"Pull the other one," Vicki said playfully. "I'm a trial and a tribulation." Her fingers were very busy now, and Max sighed with deep pleasure, standing, feet apart, as she moved over him. Her caresses wisping over his skin, light as thistledown, brought relaxation to the ragged nerve end-ings and the peace of a desire that didn't have to be con-summated but could simply be enjoyed for itself.

"Your bath's drawn," she whispered. "Hop in, and I'll soap you."

"But you're all dressed," Max protested with total lack of conviction.

"Who is?" Vicki laughed softly and pulled the shift over her head in one neat movement. Clad only in brief under-garments, she pushed him imperatively into the bathroom, dropping to her knees beside the tub as he stretched, long and lazy under the water, allowing her to do for him what he had so often done for her, and quite clearly enjoying every minute of it.

"Come on, out!" Unwillingly, Vicki got to her feet, reaching for a towel. "I reserved a table at Aux Anciens Canadiens for nine o'clock. We're going to have to move, love, if you want to stick to the original plan."

With equal reluctance, Max rose from the water in a shower of drops. "You'd just about put me to sleep." He reached for the towel.

"I had?" Vicki queried, gazing fixedly at one part of his anatomy that didn't look at all sleepy.

"Get your dress on again, wicked one! I am in sore need of my dinner and refuse to yield to temptation." Laughing, Vicki returned to the bedroom. She slipped back into her dress and was pulling a brush through her disheveled hair, wondering whether she needed makeup after all, when Max asked her a question.

"Did you book a return flight? Another two days here should be enough for me."

"I didn't notice, actually," she responded casually. "Lois booked my ticket—I expect she left the return open. You can check if you like. My travel stuff is all in the drawer under the desk."

She saw him in the mirror as he went through her documents, saw the incredulous look on his face and her heart plummeted with a sickening thud.

"What the hell is this, Victoria?" Max thrust the folder holding her ticket under her nose.

"What it looks like, I guess," she responded with an attempt at lightness.

"You just told me Lois arranged your travel," Max said tautly, his blue eyes narrowing into icy slits as she turned to face him. "She would never have booked this!"

"She did because I asked her to. She was in such a state after your somewhat precipitate departure that I thought it would give her something else to think about." Vicki examined his expression nervously. He was clearly very angry— she'd seen an occasional flash of temper before, but never this degree of rawness. With anyone else, it wouldn't have alarmed her, but Max had never made any secret about the probable consequences of his anger. She sought desperately for something to say to avert whatever it was she should avert, but, as she watched his face, the most extraordinary thing happened. Max drew into himself, almost visibly wiping all trace of emotion from his expression. The ice faded from the blue eyes, which instead reflected simply a blank—total nothingness.

"Would you give me your definition of marriage?" It was his normal voice—and yet it wasn't. Something fundamental was missing, and Vicki began to shake as a miasma of cold hugged her in a clammy, invincible, fog-laden hold.

"Look, darling, this was my impulse, my trip, my expense . . ." she began miserably.

"I asked you for your definition of marriage," Max interrupted roughly.

"Two people, committing themselves to each other, deciding that they need each other for completion," she said softly. It was the best she could manage when put on the spot in this impossible fashion.

"And doesn't that include the concept that what's yours is mine and what's mine is yours?" Max demanded.

"Does it? I don't know . . . I haven't really thought about it." She had, of course, but was incapable of coherent thought or articulation under the hard voice and relentless gaze.

"Then think about it!" He grasped her shoulders, and for a fleeting instant the anger was there again, only to be wiped out by some deep, inner control that was more frightening than anything she had ever seen.

"Let's get one thing straight, Victoria, once and for all. I will *not* have a different lifestyle from my wife's—yours, to be precise. And since I am *not* prepared to change my lifestyle to fit in with your preference for a bohemian and totally unnecessary financial independence, *you* are going to have to compromise on this one!"

Vicki hovered on the brink of saying, "And if I consider that unacceptable?" She hovered, teetered, fought against a question that she knew in the deepest center of herself would produce an ultimatum that she would be forced to reject and that Max would be forced to stand by. This was too small an issue for a confrontation that would leave them both on separate cliffs, waving forlornly at each other over the vast chasm of intransigence.

"I yield," she said quietly, definitely.

The silence in the room elongated, the almost subliminal musical murmurings from the radio only adding to its depth and quality as they stood facing each other, so close that they should be touching, yet so far apart that they should be in separate rooms.

"Oh, green eyes, what wasteland did we nearly reach?" Max spoke, breaking the thin line of uncertainty, a hoarse, rasping note in the usually even voice.

"An unnecessary one," Vicki said gently, moving into the arms that reached to enfold her.

"Let me try and explain something." Max spoke softly, drawing her over to the bed, pulling her down beside him. "When you do things like this—" he flicked the ticket he still held—"I feel as if you're rejecting me, my values, and ultimately our marriage."

"But that's ridiculous!" she exclaimed. "I'm rejecting nothing, merely operating every now and again as an independent being. I don't see why you should pay for a flight that was entirely my impulse. If you *want* to, *have* to, I'll learn to live with it, but you have to understand something, too." She turned sideways to look at him, absorbing the gravity of his expression.

"I'm listening," he said quietly.

"This may sound strange, my love, but one of the most exciting, exhilarating experiences of my life was when I found myself without any financial cushion. Suddenly, I was having to make choices, set priorities, think about basics like food and a roof. I'd never had to do that before, and neither had anyone I'd ever met. It was a whole different world out there, and I had to learn to live by its rules and within a totally new set of constraints. But, paradoxically, it freed me, somehow." Vicki paused for a moment, playing absently with his hand. "I learned to rely only on myself and I'm having difficulty breaking the habit."

Max sighed heavily. "I'm not asking for a dependent, woolly-headed woman for a wife, Victoria. I don't want you any different from the way you are, but I *do* want you to accept the realities. It makes absolutely no sense for you to behave as if you're still an impoverished student when you aren't. We both dip into the same financial pot, and there are no distinctions between what's yours and what's mine. If you reject what I have to offer, then you are fundamentally rejecting me."

"I think you're being just a little simplistic," Vicki said quietly but without rancor. "However, I accept the realities. I didn't marry you with my eyes closed." She smiled slightly and noted his valiant attempt at an answering smile. "I knew what I was doing and never expected it to be easy—but we both have our habits and they die hard."

"I want this one dead and buried," Max stated bluntly.

"Be patient, my love, there's not much life left in it." Raising his hand, she kissed the palm, rubbing it over her face. "You are, of course, quite the most patient person I've ever come across." In the ensuing silence, he wrapped her tightly in his arms and they clung to each other, without passion but with the hungry need for reconciliation.

After a while, Vicki pulled herself upright. She had one more point to make before this messy business was put back in Pandora's box.

"You were angry, Max, but you wouldn't let yourself be. I would never court your anger, or anyone else's for that matter—it's far too ugly an emotion—but . . ." Vicki bit her lip, "but at least it's an emotion and I can relate to it. When you withdrew like that, I just felt like . . . like . . . a speck of dust that has to be swept away," she finished with a sigh.

There was a long silence—there had been a lot of those in the last hour—and then Max spoke quietly. "Victoria, what you saw was not me *controlling* my anger, but the anger itself. I've told you that Randalls express those feelings rather differently from Carroltons. We don't have brief shouting matches that end with kiss-and-make-up, we create icy wastes that stretch into infinity. If you hadn't pulled me back from the edge, we'd still be in that frigid zone now, and I wouldn't be able to do a damn thing about it and neither would you."

Vicki got to her feet with brisk resolution, standing in front of him, hands resting determinedly on her hips. "We all have our faults, husband, but I'm telling you that this one of yours is going to have to change. You're going to have to learn to yell like ordinary people—do you understand?"

"Don't you talk to me like that, you fierce little virago!" Max exclaimed on a shout of laughter, seizing her hands and jerking her forward to fall in an ungainly heap on the bed. Vicki struggled to turn over, laughing helplessly, squirming under his ruthless hands as he tickled her into gasping submission.

"Oh, it's not fair," Vicki got out, rolling onto her back when he eventually released her. "I can't help being ticklish and you shouldn't take advantage."

"Don't ask for it, then," Max told her with mock severity.

"You are now an utter mess, my love. Your mascara's all smudged and your dress is hopelessly wrinkled. You can't possibly go out for dinner in that condition."

"Well, whose fault is that?" Vicki retorted, getting to her feet. "I didn't get myself into this state."

"No, but you're going to get yourself out of it," he noted equably. "See to your face and I'll find you something else to wear."

One wasteland averted, Vicki reflected as she creamed her face thoughtfully. She was just going to have to be on the watch for future ones. Now that she knew the signs, it would be easier; she simply had to learn how to step in instantly at the right moment. She felt an odd thrill of pleasure and challenge. This was the nitty-gritty of marriage; the dreamland of courtship and the idyll of the early months laid a foundation but were not sufficient unto themselves. She and Max had a lifetime to share and, as time progressed, would find each other's rough edges. The fording could be . . . no, *would* be . . . painful, but each would learn how to smooth the jagged corners of the other and how to smooth their own to an acceptable, workable surface.

Vicki emerged from the bathroom, walked to her husband, and gently put her arms around him. "Will you learn with me, my love?"

"I'll be pacing you every step of the way, my own wife," Max affirmed quietly, and she relaxed against him, filled with a peaceful joy.

 9

On a sunny evening several weeks later, Max very quietly

let himself into the house, his arms fully occupied with a very large wicker basket that showed a curious tendency to move of its own accord. He put it down carefully just inside the door, a smile of gleeful anticipation curving his mouth.

"Anyone home?" he called cheerfully.

"In the kitchen," came his wife's shouted response. "You'll have to come to me, I'm in the middle of something I can't leave." There was a note of laughter in her voice that narrowed his eyes, drew a slight, puzzled but interested frown between the thick eyebrows. She was clearly up to something, and that, Max reflected, made two of them.

He pushed through the swinging door into the kitchen and stood for a moment in total amazement, before a shout of laughter rocked the room. "Victoria Randall! How could you? I have never seen such an erotic sight! Suppose I had brought someone home with me?"

"I called Lois to check," she informed him serenely, turning from the stove with an utterly mischievous grin. "Come try this sauce—it may need more salt."

Keeping his hands firmly at his sides, Max crossed the room, his eyes dancing as laughter and desire fought for precedence.

"What do you think?" She held a wooden spoon to his lips.

"I think . . ." Max murmured, licking the spoon, "that when a man walks into his kitchen to find his wife stark naked except for a ridiculous apron, busily concocting a taste of heaven, perhaps she's trying to tell him something?" His eyebrows lifted as he continued, with considerable effort, to keep his hands to himself.

"You could be right," Vicki said demurely. "What do you

think she might be trying to say?"

"Well, now," Max drawled, eyelids drooping, "perhaps that she's sorry for being such a grouch this morning?"

Vicki laughed softly. "I *was* horrid—I'm sorry."

Max shook his head slightly. "I was not exactly even-tempered myself, or I might have been able to do something about you. But I detest oversleeping!"

"I can't imagine how I happened to turn off the alarm," Vicki murmured ruefully, standing on tiptoe to reach her arms around his neck. "I didn't do it consciously."

His hands ran down the length of her bare back, deftly untying her apron strings, then slid to her front, smoothing over her belly, whispering upward over the tautened skin of her ribcage to mold her breasts in his palms.

"If this is the reception I get after a morning tiff, maybe we should quarrel more often."

Vicki chuckled, rubbing herself against his length, smiling with pleasure as he hardened under her touch. "Shall we go on to the next stage of the reception? I've always had a slight hankering for the kitchen table." Her eyes glowed as her fingers went to work on his shirt buttons.

"You are such an unpredictable, exciting creature, green eyes," Max murmured, and then, with a sudden exclamation, seized her hands. "No, we can't! At least not just yet."

"Why ever not?" Vicki regarded him in puzzled disappointment.

"I have a present for you that won't wait." He grinned wickedly. "But you're going to have to put something on, other than an apron, to open it."

"I do not need any more presents, Max Randall," she

stated firmly. "You're a compulsive present-giver—at this rate you'll be a founding member of Gift-givers Anonymous!"

"Stay here and I'll fetch you a robe. You're not to move from this room, understand?"

"My feet are glued to the floor." Vicki watched him leave the room with the long, precipitate stride that characterized his movements during these enthusiasms. His presents were not only frequent, they were always imaginative—not necessarily expensive, but always appropriate and interesting. Vicki had often wondered how he found the time in his hectic schedule both to come up with the ideas and to put them into practice. She had finally come to the conclusion that one could always find time for what one really wanted to do and that giving pleasure was an integral component of her husband's personality.

Vicki turned back to the stove, checking the Madeira sauce that would accompany their tournedos—if they ever got that far this evening! What with present-giving and what she had in mind for afterward, it looked unlikely. She jumped as Max's hand, cool and proprietorial, came to rest on her bottom. He'd crept on cat's feet across the sound-absorbent cork tiles and laughed softly at her startled reaction.

"You can't expect to offer such blatant invitations without their being taken up, my sexy little love."

"Guess not." Vicki swung around with a grin. "I'd be *very* disappointed if they weren't."

"Put this on—my present is getting very impatient and I'm afraid there'll be a disaster if you don't open it soon." Max maneuvered her arms into the sleeves of the long cotton caftan, zipped it from hem to throat with one brisk movement, and nodded with satisfaction. "All sealed up, you are rather less of a temptation—not much less, but enough to allow me to deal with the necessities."

Vicki gurgled at his matter-of-fact tone that was quite at odds with the purple hue of those usually bright blue eyes. With an imperious hand on the hollow of her back, he propelled her out of the kitchen and into the hall. She looked at the enormous, squirming basket.

"What on earth is it?"

"Take a look." Max laughed delightedly at her astounded expression as she crossed the warm, waxed floor, bent, and with some trepidation lifted the lid.

"Max! What is it?" A pair of huge, soulful brown eyes regarded her hopefully and an enormous tail thumped as a rough-coated, brindle and white creature scrambled ungracefully out of the basket. It behaved like a puppy, but was far bigger than any puppy Vicki had ever seen. Four huge paws skittered on the polished floor as it pranced around her, a large, very wet pink tongue licking her bare feet before it turned its attention to Max's shoelaces.

"It's a St. Bernard," Max announced on a choke of laughter. "But, actually, it's 'she,' not 'it.' "

"What are we going to do with it. . . . I mean she . . . no, her?" Victoria was aghast. She had been raised with dogs, but had never seen any of that species quite this huge.

"She's yours," Max said simply, dropping to caress the floppy ears as the oversized puppy beamed breathily at him.

"Oh, Lord!" Vicki absorbed this. "How old is it . . . she?"

"Eight and a half weeks."

"That's all? Max, she's going to be massive!"

"Between a hundred forty and a hundred seventy pounds," he said cheerfully. "When she's all grown up."

"Oh, dear." Vicki dropped cross-legged to the floor and clicked her fingers. The puppy jumped delightedly into her lap, nearly knocking her backward as the huge head leveled with hers.

"Don't you like her?" Max asked the question with such a look of little-boy anxiety on his face that she burst out laughing.

"Yes, of course I do, darling. Only . . . only . . ." Vicki gave up. "What are we going to call her?"

"She already has some elaborate breeding name that I can't recall—it's in the documents somewhere. But we'll have to find something a little more domestic."

"Talking of domestic," Vicki observed carefully, "I think whoever-she-is just needed a bush."

Max surveyed the spreading puddle with a rueful grin. "I'll clean up if you'll take her outside."

"It's a case of locking the stable door after the horse has bolted, but I suppose it's never too late to learn cause and effect." The puppy was too big to lift easily, so Vicki shooed it out of the front door with an imperative toe and a growl in her voice. "She" appeared totally unconcerned, and rushed across the sweep of green lawn toward the trees bordering the lane before turning with excited yelps to invite Vicki to play. The invitation was irresistible and, with a mental shrug of amused resignation, Vicki reconciled herself to the large, demanding presence of this other in her life.

"Don't you think she's entrancing?" Max appeared at her elbow with two frosted glasses of white wine, and they stood for a few moments watching the gambols of the ungainly youngster.

"Very entrancing," Vicki said after a while, "but I still haven't worked out what I'm going to do with her all day—and what Josefa is going to say about an unhousebroken, elephantine puppy making her mark all over the house. Those rugs, my love, won't take too much punishment."

"I hadn't thought that far ahead." His fingers slipped up the column of her neck. "I'll take her back tomorrow . . . it's just that I thought . . . oh, never mind, golden girl, it was a ridiculous impulse and, I see now, quite impractical. She goes in the morning."

"What did you think?" Vicki turned her head under the stroking fingers. She hadn't the slightest intention of rejecting his gift, although the realities of living with this creature were clearly more obvious to her than they were to Max, but she wanted to know why he'd had such an idea.

"I don't like the idea of you being all alone," he said simply. "I know you like to be without human distractions, but it still bothers me, particularly when I'm away, to think of you up in that studio at all hours with no living presence around you." He sighed suddenly. "I'm sorry, Victoria. This wasn't a present for you, it was actually for me—I didn't mean to be selfish."

Warm, overpowering love mixed with the overwhelming knowledge of being loved suffused her. Her bones became feathers in the wind as her blood thinned, all the better to dance and sing as she reached for him—for Max, for her husband, who was at this moment so vulnerable, so loving, so anxious that his love be returned. At this moment, he was just like the young, would-be lovers on the banks of the Hudson that her swift pencil had captured all those weeks ago, in a July when the autumnal turning of the leaves had seemed an eon away.

"My own love, every moment that Milady is with me will be a moment when I know that I am with you in spirit." It was a soft statement; she held him quietly and let the declaration lie, sufficient unto itself.

"Milady is a very dainty name for such a gangling creature," Max said quietly, following the overt direction of their conversation although his hold indicated clearly that he was on the covert wavelength.

"She'll grow into it." Vicki opened his shirt and gently nibbled his soft pink nipples. "How about we feed her and let her play in the paddock while we go on to step two of the reception committee?"

Vicki awoke bemused in the black darkness of the night—noises of pathetic desolation filled her ears. She shot upright at the same instant that Max turned on his bedside light.

Vicki stated the obvious. "She's unhappy."

"She will be for a few nights, love. She's not used to sleeping alone."

"Well, perhaps we should—"

"No!" His sharp exclamation interrupted her. "I will *not* share a bedroom with anyone but you, and if you go comfort her, she'll never learn."

Vicki lay down again, gazing wide-eyed into the renewed darkness as the plaintive wail filled her head, stirred her body. "It's no good, Max. I accept what you say, but I can't lie here and listen to this. It's as bad as a hungry baby!"

The light flicked on again and Max leaned on his elbow.

"Do you think I could have one of *those* for my birthday?"

Suddenly, Vicki could no longer hear the yelps from the kitchen as she looked up into the sleepy but intense face hanging over her. "Your birthday's only three months away—I work fast, my darling, but not that fast."

"Forget the timing—how about the principle?"

"I'm not sure." She wanted to say, "Why do we have to discuss this now? Why are you springing this on me in the middle of the night, for heaven's sake?" But those heavy, anxiously questioning, love-filled eyes smothered the questions.

"I've been so busy creating paintings that I haven't thought about babies," she said instead. "You don't think learning to be married is enough for the time being?"

"How long is it going to take us to learn?" A crescendo of cries from downstairs broke the intense concentration and, in a strange way, gave Vicki her answer.

"Let's deal with *that* infant first, and plan on next birthday for the human variety. By that time, we should be experts at this marriage business."

"I have a strange feeling, my own, that one never becomes an expert—the software gets more advanced and there's always a new program to learn." Max drew her beneath him, his body heavy on hers as she lifted to receive him and they moved through the thicket of absolute togetherness that they both understood and that could admit of no separation.

The October light coming through the skylight was crisp and clear, illuminating the studio and the series of canvases—for once, turned to face the room—with sharp, white clarity. The concentrated silence of the four people was an almost palpable force as they examined the body of work that constituted three years of Vicki's working life. Everyone in the room had seen each painting individually, but this was the first time that anyone but Vicki had examined them collectively.

Dan stopped before the three paintings that were pivotal to the creative process of those years and that would provide the focus for the Washington show, scheduled to open in two weeks. He said nothing, but a long, bony arm came to rest on her shoulders and Vicki felt some of the expectant, anxious rigidity leave her body. While she trusted Max's judgment of her work, he was not an expert and would not pretend to be one, and, while she trusted her own judgment, working so intensely and in such close contact could cloud objectivity. Only Dan could be the final arbiter—he knew her as a painter better than anyone, knew what she was capable of and what he and the art world wanted and expected of her.

Max watched the wordless exchange with the slightest pang of what he recognized disgustedly was jealousy. Dan could give his wife something that he could not—something that had to do with her working self, a judgment that she trusted implicitly. Max could tell her how much he liked a painting, could talk knowledgeably about why, and she would trust his statements . . . but always with the unspoken qualification that they were essentially subjective. Dan shared a part of her, knew a part of her, that Max did not. It was neither reasonable nor logical to be threatened by their closeness, but the demon of jealousy still required a leash.

Milady abandoned the patch of sunlight where she had

been basking, watching this curious group of humans, absorbing the atmosphere of tension and expectancy with the resigned bemusement of her kind, and padded toward Max, her instincts apparently telling her that he needed attention. She sat at his feet, whining insistently, demanding his attention because it was the only way she knew how to confer her own. Max lifted and kneaded the thick, loose fold of skin around the puppy's neck with a soft smile of recognition. She was, without question, Victoria's dog, but she had come to him in his moment of need.

Vicki turned away from Dan's confirming arm as she heard Milady's whine and took in the scene instantly. As she looked at Max, he raised his head and gave her a small, self-deprecating smile that said everything. She blew him a kiss, then turned briskly to Dan.

"So, Mr. Kesselbaum, what think you?" Her tone was light, cheerful, sending the gravity of the last half-hour scuttling into the shadows.

"I think, Vicki Carrolton, that you are about to throw D.C. back on its heels," Dan stated decisively. "What do you think, Bev?"

The young woman turned toward Vicki, her large brown eyes curiously watery. "I'm overwhelmed," she said simply. "I've never seen anything quite so disturbing, so painful, so . . . so powerful as these holocaust paintings. I don't know how you could depict that and . . . well, and still stay sane." She looked at the others in frustration. "Does anyone understand what I mean?"

"Absolutely," Max said quietly. "However," he smiled suddenly, "I can vouch for Victoria's sanity, although there are times when I doubt my own!" He came to stand behind her, wrapping her with his arms, and she leaned back against his long body, absorbing his thoughts and anxieties as she melded into him, offering reassurance.

"I'm going to check on lunch, Dan. Why don't you and Bev do your cataloguing and whatever else it is that you do."

"Fine." Dan scratched his nose, becoming instantly businesslike. "Everything I see is to go—right?"

"Everything that's facing outward," Vicki defined carefully. "You can look at the other stuff if you like, but save your breath if you want any of it, because it isn't going anywhere!"

"All right, Vicki." Dan chuckled. "I learned that lesson the hard way, many years ago!"

"It still doesn't stop you from trying, though!" Vicki gave him an affectionate slap on her way to the door. Milady shot between her legs in the excitement of the prospect of a change of scene, and Vicki fell backward, laughing, into Max's waiting arms. "One of these days, that dog's going to give someone a broken leg!"

"She still hasn't learned to cope with her feet." Max chuckled. "They seem to have difficulty going in the same direction at the same time." Laughing, they went down to the kitchen, leaving Dan and Bev to their work.

"Did you have a problem up there?" Vicki asked calmly, beginning to set the table.

"You guessed, huh?" Max shrugged ruefully. "Let's drop it—I'm feeling silly enough as it is."

"So you should," Vicki declared roundly. "I don't get bothered when I see you engaged in an intense conversation that I can't join, with some devastating lady executive who knows all about 'bulling and bearing' and whatever else."

"Drop it, golden girl!" His hand snaked out, twisted in the chignon massed at the top of her head.

"Don't get mad at *me,* Max Randall," Vicki demanded, trying to wriggle out of his hold.

"I'm not mad at you, I'm mad at myself. Keep still—you don't want a bald spot!"

"Oh, you outrageous man!" Her halfhearted protest died as he bent to kiss her neck, bringing goose bumps to shivering life on her flesh. His hand released the top of her head to run down her back, pushing up her black cashmere sweater before insinuating itself into the tight waist of her jeans. His long fingers slid down over the warm flesh of her buttocks, squeezing firmly as they reached farther with the sure knowledge of an explorer going over familiar ground.

"Max, stop it," Vicki whispered in faint protest. "Dan and Bev will be down any minute."

"We'll hear them," Max reassured against her neck. "Didn't you once talk about the kitchen table?"

"No! I mean, yes! But not with the house full of people!" In this mood, her husband was impossible and unstoppable, and her own excitement was too powerful to be put on hold as she was pushed inexorably backward until the edge of the table prevented further progress.

"Max, by the time we hear them it'll be too late!" She was laughing helplessly as he stripped off her jeans and pants with urgent fingers and dealt as swiftly with his own clothes, but she made no move to stop him as the wonderfully illicit quality of their activity heightened her excitement to an uncontrollable peak.

"Brace yourself," Max whispered imperatively. Vicki

leaned back, resting her weight on the heels of her hands pressed to the surface of the table as he raised her legs, clamping them around his waist, driving deep within her, laughing eyes melting into pools of purple-hued mercury as they fused with hers. She was unable to initiate anything with her own body, but danced with joyous laughter as he held her ankles at his back and brought them both, with the speed of necessity, to a gasping, hilarious, totally *married* finale.

"Abominable man!" Vicki slid to the floor with an exhalation of pure pleasure. "What on earth possessed you?"

"The need to confirm possession," Max said airily.

"The *what?*" Vicki exclaimed indignantly. "Of all the chauvinistic . . ." The sound of voices upstairs cut her off in midsentence. "Oh, help," she muttered, grabbing up her clothes and scuttling across the kitchen in the direction of the bathroom at the back of the house.

"Such a pretty little bottom," Max murmured at her retreating back.

"Oh, do stop it! You're nothing but a satyr," Vicki accused on a bubble of mirth, whisking herself out of the room.

When Dan and Bev appeared, chattering like a pair of sparrows, Vicki and Max were a demure, married couple, but they both shook with laughter at the most inconvenient moments and Vicki found it impossible to keep her hands off her husband as she moved with an attempt at businesslike efficiency around the kitchen. Her fingers seemed to have a life of their own as they covertly ran over his bottom, pinched his ribs, slid wickedly between his thighs.

Dan was far too high on his own egotistical cloud to notice any of this, and consumed his lunch with absentminded enthusiasm as he discussed logistics of the coming show. Bev, with her usual peaceful smile, responded to questions, offered advice, and remained her serene, imperturbable self.

It was early evening before they left, and Vicki knew that something she detested but had to face was on a fast ski slope to the end. Her work would be crated next week and would then cease to be hers. Once it had left her studio, it would sink or swim on the tide of qualified opinion and she had to let go.

"I have to warn you about something," she said quietly as they closed the door on the October dusk after waving their guests out of sight down the drive.

"Oh?" Max put his arm around her shoulders, walking her out of the central hall and into the tranquil sitting room. "Warn away, my love."

"Well . . ." Vicki snapped her thumbnail between her teeth and caught Max's sudden frown. "It's all right, I'm not really biting my nails." She paced around the room for a minute while he sat calmly, watching her. "Look," she said eventually, "I'm probably going to be fairly impossible until after the opening . . ."

"That's all right," Max interrupted with a smile. "I'm prepared for it."

"How could you know?" Vicki exclaimed. "You've never seen me at these times."

"I've lived with you for two years, green eyes." He smiled gently. "I'm getting to know what to expect."

"I'll try really hard, darling, but I can't promise that I won't . . . oh, that I won't be utterly horrid to you at times—but it won't be personal," Vicki finished with a sigh of resignation.

"I can promise you that I won't take it personally." Max crooked a finger and she came across the room, then dropped onto his knee under the compelling hand at her waist. "But I can also promise you," he went on coolly, "that if you get too outrageous, I won't indulge you."

"On the principle that to do so would simply reinforce the behavior?" Vicki queried with a slight laugh, nibbling his ear with great concentration.

"Exactly! I shall, however, be *understanding* at all times, if not indulgent—fair enough?"

"Fair enough. I give you permission to be whatever you consider appropriate, whenever." Vicki rested her head on his shoulder as Max held her with gentle confirmation. She knew herself very well, knew how she was going to feel over the next few weeks. On similar occasions in the past, she had been free to allow the feelings full rein—there had been no one else sharing her life in such closeness that they could be hurt or upset by the irritation and withdrawal that were the inevitable concomitants of her tension as she struggled to separate herself from her work. Now, she was no longer a free agent. She was going to have to accept that and everything that went with it.

❦ 10 ❦

The place was so empty! Vicki stood in the middle of her studio looking helplessly around. The packers had just completed their task, and she had waved forlornly at the departing van before retracing her steps upstairs. It was ridiculous to feel this sense of loss! But somehow, scolding herself didn't do any good—she always answered back!

The remedy, of course, was to start work again immediately, but anything serious she attempted would be a waste of time and effort until after the opening, when the separation would be complete. Two large, hot tears rolled slowly down the sides of her nose and she sniffed with cross misery.

"Oh, dear!"

Vicki whirled at the soft voice. "Max! What are you doing home?"

"I had a feeling you'd be suffering from the empty-nest syndrome. Seems I was right." Max crossed the room with a gentle smile and took her firmly into his arms. "Cry it out, golden girl, and then I'll tell you what we're going to do."

"I don't really need to cry." Vicki sniffed vigorously, pulling his handkerchief out of his breast pocket and burying her face in its clean, starchy smell. "I'm just being silly. If you're going to be sympathetic, you'll just make matters worse."

"I'll be the judge of that," Max responded peremptorily. "This is one situation where I'm going to be very controlling and I'll brook no arguments. If I tell you to cry, you'll cry."

The watery chuckle that greeted his statement brought a satisfied curve to his lips. "Now, my love, you are going to close up here until after the show. Do whatever you have to, but do it right now and very quickly."

"I'm fine now, darling." Vicki lifted her head from its comfortable resting place on his chest and struggled to pull herself out of his embrace. It was an unsuccessful struggle that she gave up rather rapidly.

"Are you leaving here on your own two feet?" Max inquired conversationally. "Because, if so, you'd better start now."

"All right, love," Vicki declared. "You've made your, point, but this has gone quite far enough. We'll go and fix some lunch, and then you can go back to the office and I'll start work."

"Oh, well, have it your own way," Max said cheerfully, and, before she could even guess what he was about to do, scooped her up behind the knees and tossed her effortlessly over his shoulder.

"Put me down, you outrageous bully!" Vicki quivered with laughter, feeling the broad shoulder beneath her shake in response as he strode out of the room, pausing to close the door with a decisive finality before continuing down the stairs to the kitchen.

Once there, he set her firmly on her feet, and Vicki eyed the door to the hall thoughtfully, imps of mischief dancing in her eyes.

"You do, my love . . ." Max left the rest of his sentence unfinished, going over to the refrigerator to take out a bottle of Gewurztraminer.

"And what . . . ?" Vicki challenged with a grin.

"There's a simple way to find out," he responded smoothly, drawing the cork with an easy flex of his wrist.

Vicki decided that perhaps she wouldn't bother. "How about lunch?" She peered critically into the fridge, pulling out drawers to examine their contents. She hadn't been spending much time in the kitchen recently, and had no idea what Josefa had provided. "Oh, that's good. We've got smoked trout, cherry tomatoes, and prosciutto—a positive feast! Hey!" Vicki squawked as Max came up behind her and suddenly put his arms around her waist, jerking her bent body against him. Staggering backward, she managed to pull herself out of the fridge and upright.

"I think lunch is going to have to wait," he whispered, nipping the nape of her neck insistently.

"Not the kitchen table again, surely?" Vicki groaned with an exaggerated sigh, trying, but failing utterly, to ignore the sudden weakness, the tremors lifting her skin under his warm breath on her neck and the fingers unzipping her jeans, reaching into the soft, curly tangle as they found their playground.

"And to think you once accused *me* of having immoderate appetites," Vicki murmured quite some time later, sitting up on the kitchen floor, running a finger down the flat belly beside her.

"If you go on doing that, you'll discover just how immoderate my appetites are," Max muttered with a laziness that was not matched by the glow in the purple-hued eyes.

"Heaven forbid!" Vicki leaped to her feet in feigned alarm, dragging on her jeans with exaggerated haste. "Make yourself respectable, Max Randall!" She dropped his shorts and pants onto his stomach, remarking with a choke of laughter, "You look very funny in just your shirt and tie and socks."

"It's all your fault," he complained, staggering to his feet. "You shouldn't offer such a provocative image."

"I was only looking to see what was in the fridge," Vicki declared.

"Sure," Max concurred dryly. "Do it again while I pour

the wine—that way I won't need to look at you."

Vicki gurgled with laughter and swiftly pulled out the makings of their lunch, setting everything on the table, then sat down to regard him thoughtfully as she took a slow sip of the fruity California wine. "What's this mysterious agenda of yours, husband?" She had come to the conclusion that Max had not really been playing a game up in her studio—he had certainly behaved as if he had something definite in mind.

"Well, now, green eyes." He smiled, neatly filleting the trout and placing a large slice on her plate. "Where would you like to spend the next week?"

Vicki squeezed lemon on the fish and frowned. What was he up to now? "Outer Mongolia," she announced calmly.

"It's a long way to go for a week, but if that's what you really want . . . ?" He reached for the cordless phone on the counter behind him.

"No, of course I don't," Vicki choked. "Are you serious?"

"Utterly. We are going away tonight—anywhere you wish—and we won't come back to this house until after Washington. I'm giving you the choice of *where* we go— but that's the only choice you have," Max added with that wicked grin.

"Lucky me!" Vicki shook her head slightly. This was so absolutely, typically, Max. He saw a potential problem and thought of a way to avoid it. He couldn't have picked a better way, she thought, abandoning her lunch to go around the table and position herself firmly on his knee.

"Can you leave the office for a week?" Her hands stroked the unruly thatch of black hair, kneading the strong column of his neck to express her gratitude.

"Sure," he responded, encircling her waist with one arm as he continued his meal with the other. "But it would be easier if you picked somewhere remotely civilized—with a phone, if you see what I mean?"

"Not to mention a telex." Vicki chuckled, diverting his fork into her own mouth.

"It would help," he agreed matter-of-factly. "If you're going to eat *my* lunch, perhaps I should eat yours."

"Oh, how I love you, Max Randall." Vicki pulled his head around with imperative hands and kissed him hungrily, catching his lower lip between her teeth, sucking with all the desperate thirst of a lost wanderer in the Sahara.

Max groaned and yielded his mouth willingly to the demanding one above, and for long moments they remained joined as his hands pushed up and under the wool sweater, fingers warm on her spine, dancing over her skin. At last he pulled back, maneuvered her to the farthest extremity of his lap, and demanded, "Where to, golden girl?"

"Mexico," Victoria announced promptly. "Much more appealing than Outer Mongolia, don't you think?"

"Definitely. All right, then, Mexico it is. Now, get off my knee and finish your lunch while I arrange things." Vicki stood up with a laugh and resumed her own seat, watching as Max briskly reached for the phone, had a brief exchange with Lois, and then calmly continued his meal.

By six o'clock that evening they were on a flight to Mexico City. Living with Max Randall, Vicki decided complacently, was frequently an unpredictable business, but never an uncomfortable one. When he decided to take matters into his own hands, he was both unstoppable and utterly competent. She spent the next seven days finding that every half-articulated desire of hers was instantly acted upon. While Max was totally in control of the proceedings, they did everything that she wanted to do.

It was only on the flight home that Vicki fully realized that her husband had not once expressed a preference, not once grimaced at the hundredth excursion through the hundredth museum, not once asked for an afternoon on the beach, had driven cheerfully for miles across the Mexican plateau, following her inclinations, entering into her enthusiasms as if they were, indeed, his own. The fact that they were only partially so had been subjugated to *her* needs.

They flew from Mexico to Washington, bypassing the Croton house as Max had insisted they should, ignoring her mutterings that clothes for Mexico were not suitable for the end of October in D.C.

"I haven't had a shopping spree for quite a while, green eyes," Max declared. "I'm looking forward to dressing you for the opening."

"What are you going to put on me?" Vicki ran a daring hand up his thigh as they winged their way across the continent.

"At this point, I'm more interested in what I'm going to take off you," he murmured back, guiding her hand.

"May I offer you a cocktail?" The flight attendant stood smiling politely beside Max's aisle seat.

Vicki wondered whether it would be more noticeable to leave her hand where it was or to move it abruptly. She chose, instead, to lean over Max and started scrabbling under his seat as if in desperate search for some missing object.

"Champagne, please, for both of us," Max responded

coolly to the attendant's question, placing a flat palm on his wife's back, which lay across his knees. "What have you lost, darling?"

"My book." Victoria righted herself hastily, cheeks flushed, eyes dancing, to take the glass handed to her by the hopefully oblivious attendant. "I expect it's still in my purse. I just thought I'd taken it out."

"You seem to be having problems with your short-term memory," Max observed gravely as the attendant moved up the aisle.

"Ungrateful man!" Vicki choked. "I was only trying to hide your very obvious problem!"

"Since *you* created the problem in the first place, it seems only reasonable that you should deal with the consequences," he noted equably, sipping his champagne.

"I won't do it again, since it's clearly unappreciated." Vicki sat back in the wide seat with an air of unconcern.

"I was under the impression that because it *was* appreciated, you found it necessary to do a nose dive under my seat!"

At that, they both gave up the struggle for a dignified sobriety, and the remainder of the flight passed in a haze of champagne and laughter.

"Well, this may be a notorious place, but it's certainly comfortable," Victoria commented, pulling an armchair over to a window in their suite at the Watergate and sinking into it with a sigh. "Are you still behind the wheel, husband, or do I get to make some plans myself?"

Max chuckled, shucking off his jacket. "What do you have in mind, wife?"

"Well, since you have some people to see, I suggest that you see them tomorrow while I visit the gallery and see how Dan and Boris are mounting my babies."

"Can you do that without too much trauma?" Max asked seriously, unlocking their cases.

"Sure," Vicki responded confidently. "Now that the waiting's over, I'm just excited."

"I've only got a couple of people to see, and it's not going to be a question of tough negotiations," Max said thoughtfully. "We'll sleep late tomorrow, buy you something to wear, have an early lunch, and then . . ."

"We'll sleep *what?*" Vicki exclaimed in mock disbelief.

"You heard." Max grinned. "As I was saying, after lunch you can go to the gallery, I'll deal with my business, and then I'll pick you up at around four o'clock. Does that suit you?"

"Would it make any difference if it didn't?" Vicki inquired, eyebrows raised.

"No," he responded cheerfully. "Not really."

"So I thought."

They followed Max's plan to the letter, and he dropped her off outside the Seventh Street gallery in Washington's "art corridor" in the early afternoon before continuing on his way.

As Max climbed the steep, narrow stairs to the second-floor gallery several hours later, the sound of raised voices gave him pause. He frowned as he pushed through the doors into the foyer, where a group of caterers were setting up an elaborate bar and buffet. The sounds of an altercation were coming from a room to the right of the foyer, and there was no mistaking the voices of Vicki and Dan.

"Oh, hello, Max." Bev appeared from the gallery opening off to the left, looking less unflappable than usual.

"What's going on?" He gestured with his head toward the noise.

"Oh, Dan and Vicki are having a row," Bev responded matter-of-factly. "It's fairly standard at times like these. I just keep out of the way and let them get on with it."

"Well, I think perhaps *I* won't," Max declared, turning to the right.

There were three people in the cluttered office. One of them was a tall, sandy-haired man whom Max assumed was Boris Colerain, the owner of the gallery. He was looking with a degree of puzzled amusement at the other two irate individuals. Vicki, hands jammed into the side pockets of her brown wool skirt, every inch of her diminutive figure radiating fury, was dancing on her toes in front of the equally furious figure of Dan, who towered above her. No one seemed to notice Max's arrival. Max glanced quickly around the room, saw what he wanted, and moved quickly. Picking Vicki up by her tiny waist in midsentence, he deposited her firmly on top of a large filing cabinet, holding her securely in an encircling arm.

A stunned silence filled the room, and then was broken by a snort of laughter from Dan. He found himself on the receiving end of a chilly stare, and coughed awkwardly.

"Get me off here, Max, it's all dusty," Vicki finally requested, calmly enough.

Max lifted her down immediately, dusting off the back of her skirt with a degree of enthusiasm that Vicki decided ruefully was not strictly necessary.

"Now, just what was all that about?" he asked.

"It's perfectly simple," Vicki declared. "I just wanted Dan to change the position of a couple of paintings, and he won't."

"Vicki!" Dan exclaimed. "That is a *gross* distortion of the truth. The fact is, Max, that Boris and I had hung all the pictures by lunchtime, after working like galley slaves all morning, and then Vicki appears and wants to change a couple—she *said.* Obligingly, we did so, and then a couple turned into all of them, and now she says she preferred them the way they were originally and wants us to put them back again!"

"Oh, Victoria!" Max said reproachfully, though his shoulders shook slightly beneath his gray flannel jacket.

"It sounds awful when you put it like that." Vicki grimaced, scratching her freckled nose. "But how could I know they were in the right place if I didn't try them elsewhere?"

"You could, perhaps, have trusted our judgment." Boris spoke for the first time, laughter rippling in his quiet voice.

Vicki sighed. "I'm sorry. I've been a real pain, haven't I?"

"Yes," Dan agreed bluntly. There was a short silence, and then suddenly both he and Vicki burst out laughing. As Max watched, shaking his head in resigned amusement, Dan caught Vicki in a fierce hug. "Well, at least that's over for *this* time," he gasped eventually. "And you won't have another show for a few years, so we should be all right for a while."

"This happens *every* time?" Boris exclaimed. "I wish someone had warned me."

"I forgot," Bev chimed in from the doorway. "Boris, the caterers are confused about how many cases of white wine you ordered."

"I'll come and sort it out," Boris said with a sigh, distractedly running a hand through his sandy hair.

"I think the most useful service *I* can render at this point is to remove you from the scene of the crime," Max teased, running a long finger over Vicki's mouth. "Where's your coat?"

"I'll get it. It's in the closet," Dan offered so promptly that renewed laughter rippled around the room.

Vicki shrugged herself into her coat with a smile of thanks as Dan held it for her; then, standing on tiptoe, she gave him a light, apologetic kiss. "Sorry, love."

"Me, too," Dan responded. "I wasn't exactly helpful, under the circumstances. I ought to know by now what a strain this business is for you."

"Well, we're going to do something about that strain, right now," Max announced firmly, taking his wife's hand. "You need a stiff drink and a nap, Victoria. Goodbye, everyone. We'll see you all this evening." So saying, he ushered Vicki out of the office and down to the street where his cab, meter running, was still patiently waiting.

"I don't know, Victoria," Max sighed, pulling her into the circle of his arm once they were ensconced on the back seat, "I let you out of my sight for a mere two hours, and you get twisted up like a coiled spring. Try and relax now, you're like an overwound clock."

"I can't help it, love," Vicki murmured, burying her head against the crisp blue shirt, feeling the warmth of his skin beneath. "The thought of all those people tonight, wandering around, peering and poking and criticizing, absolutely terrifies me."

Max squeezed her tightly in wordless comfort, running a tender hand through the curtain of light hair on his breast. Although he was trying very hard not to show it, he was very nervous himself and had no problem understanding his wife's terror. Her work was so much a part of her, so intrinsic an expression of herself, that revealing it to the critical eyes of the world must be like one of those nightmares when one finds oneself naked in a crowded room where everyone else is respectably dressed.

"Now," Max announced, when they reached their room, "I think we'll start the relaxation process with a bottle of champagne."

"Actually, there's only one way I'm going to be able to relax," Vicki murmured, watching him through narrowed eyes as he reached for the phone.

"And what's that?" Max questioned conversationally.

"Oh, you know!" Smiling, she slid her arm around the narrow waist beneath the well-cut jacket.

"Do I?" His eyebrows lifted as he turned his attention to the helpful voice at the end of the phone.

"Don't tease," Vicki whispered, pulling his shirt out of the waistband of his trousers.

Max replaced the receiver and took her hands firmly in his own large, warm ones. "Tell me, my own wife."

"Make love to me," Vicki said softly, losing herself in his gaze.

"Take off your clothes." A husky throb accompanied the directive and, under his hooded, melting regard, Vicki swiftly removed her clothes to stand in simple nakedness before him.

His eyes swept over her in a long, slow movement, but as

143

he reached for her, there was a discreet knock at the door. Room service, with the champagne! Vicki remembered. Leaving her clothes lying in a discarded, intimate heap in the middle of the floor, she dived for the bathroom, reflecting that hotel bedrooms were the most hazardous places.

Max opened the bathroom door a few minutes later, eyes alight. "All clear. Now . . . where were we?"

❦ 11 ❦

"You really don't think this outfit is just a bit outré for a formal opening?" Victoria surveyed herself critically in the long mirror, several hours later.

"It's both elegant and distinctive," Max said calmly, coming to stand behind her. "It's also *very* sexy and you look gorgeous."

The outfit was indeed all of those things, Vicki decided. The butter-soft, skintight leather pants were topped off by a white silk shirt with full sleeves and tight wrists and a wide, floppy collar unbuttoned to the deep cleft of breasts that were quite obviously unconfined—at Max's insistence, and he was quite right, she recognized. Leather boots, rolled softly to her ankles, completed a costume that gave her a gamin look while being outrageously sexy. It also made her *feel* marvelous and filled her with the sense of poised self-confidence that she had been lacking up until this minute.

"It requires just one thing more," Max said quietly, and deftly fastened around her neck a long, intricately worked gold chain that hung to the V of the shirt, gleaming dully against her skin, which still carried its peach-gold bloom of the summer sun.

Vicki lifted the necklace off her breast in wonder. "Max, my darling, it's exactly like that Inca chain we saw in Mexico City."

"It is," he affirmed quietly.

"Not *the* chain?" Vicki exclaimed.

"No." He laughed softly. "They wouldn't sell it. But it's an exact replica, and the gold is the same quality."

"I don't know what to say," Vicki stuttered helplessly. "It's just so beautiful . . . I . . . I . . . oh, Max! I haven't deserved anything this beautiful."

"My love," he murmured, burying his lips in her clean, fragrant hair, "there is nothing in this world truly beautiful enough for you. And that you are mine, my sexy, glorious genius of the sun god, is a fact I still have difficulty believing."

"You'd better believe it, husband," she whispered, turning in his arms, "because it's *never* going to change."

Max took the small face between his hands, examining it as if it were a rare gem, before he gently but firmly possessed her lips, declaring his claim as she declared her own. "We have to go," he muttered eventually. "You must be there before the crowds arrive."

Vicki nodded as her stomach tightened, then loosened, at the thought of the evening ahead. "Hold on a minute," she gasped, disappearing rapidly. "I shouldn't have drunk all that champagne," was the only explanation she could think of as she emerged from the bathroom many minutes later.

"It's not the champagne, darling," Max said calmly, holding her coat for her. "You'll be fine once things get moving."

"Let's hope so," Vicki mumbled, without too much conviction.

They arrived at the gallery to find Dan, Bev, and Boris staring at each other over glasses of champagne. Nervous expectancy hung like a cloud over the deserted gallery and did nothing to help Vicki. Dan, looking not unlike his usual scruffy self in creased evening clothes that carried the greenish tinge of disuse, kept pulling at his long, bony fingers, clicking the joints until Vicki thought she would scream—but miraculously she didn't. Bev was radiant, her coffee-cream skin glowing against her ivory silk gown. She kept up a flow of small talk that only Max responded to, but the soft voice did much to fill the silences and ease the exacerbation of their spirits.

An hour later, the place was jammed as critics, patrons, gallery-goers, and artists jostled in a variety of dress ranging from the formal to the most casual. It was quite a party, Vicki decided, all nervousness now vanished as she sipped Perrier and tried to concentrate on the various conversations she was constantly involved in while her ears were simultaneously straining to hear the unguarded comments of the serious art lovers as they examined the body of work with minute concentration.

The crowd around the holocaust paintings never seemed to diminish, and the faces of those moving away from them were troubled. Victoria nodded with silent satisfaction—it was clearly having the intended effect.

"You should have heard what I just heard." Dan spoke against her ear.

"What was that?" Vicki turned her head slightly, her hand firmly clasped in her husband's, where it had been all evening.

"Peter Dickens just pronounced judgment." Dan chuckled softly. "He said, 'If she's doing *this* now, what's she going to be doing in ten years' time?'"

Max squeezed her hand. He had clearly heard Dan's low-voiced information, although he continued to respond with calm courtesy to the excited jabber of the diamond-bedecked wife of one of Washington's most important collectors.

Victoria now relaxed completely—Peter Dickens's opinion was the one that really mattered in these circles. Both collector and critic, he led the D.C. art world.

Looking absently toward the door, she froze suddenly and then gave a cry of pleasure. "Look who's here, Max! Why didn't they let me know?" Vicki tugged her hand free and shot off across the crowded room, the throng parting before her impetuous progress like the Red Sea before the staff of Moses.

Max chuckled, watching as his wife reached the three tall figures at the door to the foyer. There was no mistaking that the Carrolton brothers and their diminutive sister were siblings. Four bright red-gold heads met as she was lost in the all-encompassing embrace of three pairs of long arms. Excusing himself politely, Max moved, at a considerably less impatient pace than his wife's, toward the door, holding back for a moment until the immediate flurry of reunion had passed.

"Max! Max!" Vicki emerged from the circle, looking somewhat rumpled. "Come say hello." She seized his hand, pulling him forward.

"I was just about to." He smiled and pinched her nose

before extending his hand to his brothers-in-law. "What a surprise!"

"It's utterly typical!" Vicki pronounced delightedly, bouncing on her toes in the unconscious method she had developed many years ago as the only way she could come anywhere near to eye level with her enormous brothers.

"Calm down, infant!" Tom chuckled. "Marriage hasn't changed you a bit. It's supposed to make you matronly and serene."

"Heaven forbid!" Max exclaimed.

"Heaven forbid!" Steve, the youngest of the three concurred, catching his sister up by the waist and twirling her around. The sudden brilliant flash of a camera froze them all. "Oh, Lord!" Steve laughed, setting her on her feet. "Now look what we've done."

"Oh, never mind them," Vicki said impatiently. "I haven't seen you for almost six months. Where are your better halves?"

"Minding hearth and home," Tom told her cheerfully. "But we bring their love, good wishes, congratulations, and anything else that's appropriate." He examined her thoughtfully. "I don't think Mother would approve of that outfit."

"She'd have to blame Max, in that case," Vicki informed him with a grin.

"She'd *never* do that," Mike said earnestly, and they all collapsed in laughter. Isobel Carrolton's adoration of her son-in-law was a family joke.

"Let's find you all a drink," Max suggested, once the paroxysms had subsided somewhat. "Victoria, my love, do try and keep your heels on the floor!"

"I would if I could, but I can't." She laughed. "It's just

so exciting."

"It is, isn't it?" Max kissed her quickly, conscious of the interested spectators around them. "You do whatever you like, my sweet."

Vicki touched his face fleetingly, her eyes shouting her love. "I'm quite calm now," she informed him seriously.

"So I see." Chuckling softly, Max eased them all toward the bar.

"Now, Vicki, give us the tour." Tom took a long, contented sip of his bourbon and the atmosphere changed, becoming instantly serious.

"Come on then," Vicki said quietly. "We start over here." She took them around the room, explaining each painting briefly and then standing back as they absorbed it—each in his own different way, she thought affectionately. Tom looked from a slight distance, his body motionless; Mike peered closely, then stood back; Steve prowled, deep frown lines between the thin, fair eyebrows. She was not anxious about their opinions—they had all been her ardent supporters from the first moment that the three-year-old Vicki Carrolton had sketched her first scene, and they had supported her through every one of the spirited battles she'd had with a mother who couldn't cope with the idea of such an unconventional daughter. They had exercised their own form of control, but had ultimately let go when she had made her final stand. From that point, the relationships had equalized, although old habits died hard on occasion, and her talent was regarded with awe by them all.

They reached the holocaust series, and Tom inhaled sharply. Max looked across at him over Vicki's head. "How?" Tom seemed to say, and Max shrugged. He didn't know, either.

Vicki felt rather than saw the wordless exchange. Max's hand was clasping the back of her neck firmly, as it had been from the beginning of the tour, and she felt his silent statement seeping through the skin beneath the warm fingers. It was wonderfully strange, she reflected, how they seemed to share thought processes almost by osmosis.

The group stopped before a small oil painting of two lovers lying under the trees on the banks of the Hudson. Vicki regarded it with all the pleasures of memory. Turning her original sketch into the painting had provided welcome relief from the intensity of the holocaust series.

"Well, if it isn't *all* the Carroltons." Dan appeared jovially beside them. "Isn't she something?" He ruffled Vicki's hair, beaming proprietorially.

"Something else altogether," Tom muttered. "Vicki, I *have* to have that."

"Of course," she said simply, lifting the small painting off the wall with her customary directness. "It's yours." She turned and held it out to him with a smile.

"Vicki! You *can't* do that!" Dan expostulated. "It's part of the show and, besides, Max has bought it."

"Max has *what?*" The color drained from her face, all life dying from her slanted green eyes as she stood encased in concrete, numbed, her blood coagulating into thick, heavy coldness. "How could you possibly have done such a thing?" She turned slowly to face her husband. "You were going to *buy* something of mine? After everything! I . . . I . . ." It was no good, there were no words. Turning, she made her way out of the thronged rooms, through the foyer, and down the stairs, where people shoehorned them-

150

selves in a frenetic column, some up, some down.

A stunned silence gripped the group by the painting. And then Max broke it. "Dear Lord! What have I done?"

"Made a *big* mistake," Tom told him succinctly. "Perhaps you don't know Carroltons yet, Max."

"Vicki has to come back," Dan announced distractedly. "The press has been promised an interview in fifteen minutes."

"We'll get her." The three brothers turned as one body.

"No!" Max's sharp negative arrested them. "This is between Victoria and myself. It was *my* error, and *I* will be the one to deal with its consequences."

"Of course," Tom agreed quietly.

Max pushed through the crowd, heedless of the startled glances drawn by his imperious, hasty progress. He ran down the stairs, ignoring the pointed comments of those he removed from his path. How could he have been so utterly, stupidly, blindly thoughtless? And he *hadn't* thought. He'd wanted to surprise her when she saw the painting hung in the spot he knew it had to fill in their bedroom. But to buy it! Tom Carrolton had just asked for it; why on earth hadn't he simply done the same? Because he still didn't understand about families! The thought pounded in his head as he stood on the sidewalk looking desperately up and down the street. Apart from the fact that it was a cold night and Vicki had left with no coat over the thin silk shirt, this was not a part of town where a woman could roam alone and in safety. His eye caught a glimmer of white at the far corner of the street, and he ran, feet thudding on the pavement, thankful for all those dogged laps in the swimming pool during the long summer months.

Vicki heard the feet behind her, recognized them in the depths of her bewildered unhappiness, thought of increasing her own speed, and dismissed the thought instantly. This was not something she could run from. She stopped, waiting for Max to reach her.

"My sweet love!" Max seized her rigid body in a convulsive grip, desperately trying to stroke some reaction from her as his hands ran over her back, tugged her curls, held her head fiercely against his chest. "Victoria, I don't know how I could have been so crassly stupid!"

"I don't either," Vicki said dully. "You buy me presents all the time, you . . . you *overwhelm* me with presents, and I accept them because I know it's something you have to do. I don't *need* them to know that you love me."

"Oh, God," he whispered desolately, holding her head so tightly that her ears began to buzz.

"When I don't want to use your money, you're hurt and feel rejected," Vicki continued. "I capitulated there, because your need was greater than mine, but how could *you* then play by different rules?" Her voice faded, and a bitter, winter-promising gust of wind whistled around the corner of the street. She shivered.

"I didn't *think.* Believe me, my darling, I just didn't *think.* I don't understand this give-and-take of families yet. I want to give and you to take—it's the only way I know to be sure that you know I love you and that you love me."

Vicki shivered again both with cold and the aftermath of distress. She heard his words and understood them; heard the desperate apology and the plea for understanding and reached for his hand, managing a feeble squeeze, although she had, as yet, no adequate words.

It was enough for Max, however. "Put this on, my dove, you're freezing." Shrugging out of his jacket, he draped it firmly around her shoulders. "No, put your arms in the sleeves, sweet love. It's warmer that way."

Vicki did as he asked, wrapping herself in his body warmth that still clung to the fine material, feeling the shivers slow and finally cease.

"Victoria, listen to me now." Max held her shoulders, knowing absolutely that what he was about to say was the only right thing to do.

"Tom must have *The Lovers.*"

"No!" Vicki whispered.

"Yes!" Max said decisively. "He wants the painting, and I couldn't handle the memories it would evoke every time I looked at it. But I want something in return."

Vicki raised her head, her body now still and quiet. "Anything," she said softly.

"I want the three holocaust paintings."

They both knew what he was asking—he was asking for the part of herself that she revealed only in her work, he was asking for the culmination of the last ten years of searching and experience, he was asking for a huge chunk of her very self. And who better to give it to?

"Where will you hang them?" Vicki asked. They certainly weren't drawing-room pieces.

"In the lobby of the Randall Corporation," Max answered readily. "They'll be seen by a great many people there."

"I'm not sure how good that will be for business." Vicki managed a small chuckle. "It's rather a case of 'Abandon hope, all ye who enter here!' "

"They should know that already." Max buried his lips in

her hair. "My love, have we sorted this one out?"

"Yes," Vicki replied, pushing her hands into the pockets of his jacket with an unthinking fervor that made Max wince slightly as he thought of the probable damage to the fabric. "But it's never to happen again—understand?"

"Understood, green eyes; that's one mistake I will never make again! But, if you *must* put your hands into pockets that weren't cut for them, do you think you could do so just a little less forcefully?" The plaintive note in his voice brought the smile that he had been longing for. "Come on, let's go back, love. You have to talk to the press."

"I guess," Vicki concurred. "I wish we could just go quietly home, though. I'm not in the mood for a question-and-answer session right now."

"You know we can't just go home," Max said quietly.

"Sure I do." Vicki laughed suddenly. "I expect poor Dan's utterly distracted! Although I have a bone to pick with him," she added. "How *could* he have taken your money?"

"Leave Dan out of this, Victoria, please," Max begged urgently. "It's just between us, and no one's to blame but me."

"I'd still like to give him a piece of my mind, though," Vicki declared grimly. "But don't worry, I won't."

It was a nervous group waiting for them as they squeezed up the narrow staircase and into the still-packed foyer. Dan, a picture of edgy distraction, pushed his way toward them.

"Thank goodness! I was beginning to think Max would never bring you back." His pale eyes suddenly sparkled. "Good news, though. Several people are interested in buying the holocaust paintings!"

"The series belongs to Max," Vicki said calmly. A sharp

inhalation ran around the group, and Tom gave a tiny, appreciative smile as he nodded at Max.

"Vicki, you can't *do* that!" Dan wailed—at the rate Vicki was going, there'd be nothing left to sell by the end of the evening.

"Dan . . ." she said quietly, holding his eyes in a firm, locked gaze.

Dan returned the look seriously for long seconds and then shrugged. "I don't think I'll ever understand you, Vicki Carrolton. But it's your business, I guess. Let's go talk to the press; Boris is getting more than a little anxious." Dan chortled suddenly. "He's been mumbling about the unpredictability of the artistic temperament ever since you disappeared in such a hurry."

"Well, you should take some responsibility for that, Daniel Kesselbaum," Vicki retorted swiftly.

"Victoria," Max broke in quickly, "I thought we had an agreement."

"We do." She flashed him a smile. "Let me go do my duty, and then, perhaps, we can get out of here."

Max nodded. "Want me to come with you?"

"No." She shook her head cheerfully. "I might decide to say something outrageous; you'll be happier if you don't hear it."

"That's our infant." Steve chuckled. "She may get older, but she never gets wiser."

Vicki's tongue peeked between her lips, her eyes dancing. "It's a Carrolton trait, brother dear." This sort of teasing banter was the preferred style of communication among the Carroltons, but it was one that could confuse outsiders. She glanced at Max—his face bore its usual expression of amusement when he was around her family. After two years, he was beginning to understand the principle and method, but it was still a foreign language to him.

"Darling, if you still need my coat, could you be careful of the contents in the inside pocket?" he requested conversationally as she turned to cross the room with Dan.

"Oh, I didn't realize I was still wearing it." Vicki stopped. "Would you like it back?"

"Not if you still need it," he replied softly.

Vicki thought for a minute. Her hands were still jammed into the pockets, her body somehow cradled in the silky material of what, on her, was a voluminous garment. "I think I do." She smiled, and Max nodded his understanding.

"Be careful of my worldly goods, then, green eyes."

He watched her as, for the next fifteen minutes, she was the focus of a group of journalists and photographers. Judging by the gales of laughter emanating from the group, she was in good form, her bright head bobbing to punctuate her remarks.

"Would you believe this?" Vicki's voice bubbled with hilarity as she rejoined them. "Some idiot actually asked me if my . . . if my . . ." she gasped through tears of laughter, "if my 'association' with Max Randall—my 'association,' if you please!—had affected my work."

"What did you say?" Mike inquired, his own voice shaking.

"Don't ask!" Dan exclaimed. "It was ribald in the extreme, and so utterly quotable, it'll be all over the *Post* tomorrow!"

"Well, my 'association'—I ask you!" Vicki declared. "It sounds like a business partnership."

"So it is, in one way," Tom observed thoughtfully. "Marriage is a business, much like any other."

Vicki frowned, her laughter fading. It was, of course—a business with its own ground rules, its own negotiating arena, its own goals, rewards and penalties, its successes and failures. Her hand slipped into the large, welcoming palm of her husband's. "In that case, husband, perhaps we should go back to the hotel and 'associate,'" Victoria murmured, eyes demurely lowered beneath curling lashes.

"Vicki, please try to keep a curb on your tongue over Thanksgiving," Tom begged, through his own merriment. "You know Mother can't cope with remarks like that."

"Oh, Max has to be away on business over Thanksgiving and I'm going with him," Vicki announced with blithe disregard for the truth.

"I do? You are?" Max inquired with a quizzical frown.

Vicki glared up at him. As she had expected, his eyes were gleaming, but there was more than a hint of reproof behind the amusement. He had quite deliberately chosen not to back up her story—she had only herself to blame, of course. She had intended to explain her plan, arrange to turn it into the truth, and then concoct a polite letter of explanation and apology to her mother as soon as they returned from D.C. Max would have respected her wishes in those circumstances, whether he wanted to or not. As it was, the unexpected arrival of her brothers this evening and then Tom's absolute assumption about the holiday had caught her unawares, and Max never appreciated being put on the spot.

"Seems like your 'association' isn't communicating too well," Tom observed dryly.

Vicki sighed. "It's just that the thought of another family

Thanksgiving, Tom, is so depressing. There hasn't been one single holiday in my memory when we've got away without a major row. I just don't want to expose Max to that." She looked around the circle of faces and saw only an impenetrable wall of disapproval. Seven years ago, faced with that wall, she would have launched into a furious defense of her right to choose her own course. Now, she acknowledged their right to disapprove of her sentiments and their right to her presence at what was the year's largest gathering of the clan. "I wasn't trying to duck out of it altogether," she said carefully. "I had hoped we could have a weekend afterward with just the immediate family—it's the aunts and uncles and cousins and great aunts and . . ."

"We'll do both," Max stated quietly.

"You don't know what you're letting yourself in for, love." Vicki sighed. "Mother gets totally hyper when the house is bursting at the seams, and guess who gets the flak?"

"Come on, Vicki," Tom said. "Steve, Mike, and I will promise to draw the fire, if you promise to take ten deep breaths before you speak. Agreed?"

"Agreed." Vicki gave them a resigned smile. They were actually far from unsympathetic and knew that she was not exaggerating the situation. Max did not yet know that— he'd only seen Isobel Carrolton at her best in the months before their wedding and on the actual day of their marriage—bright, elegant, utterly charming, reveling in the incredible prospect of her unconventional daughter's doing something, for once, absolutely according to the book. And, of course, he would enjoy the large, many-branched family gathering as much as he had enjoyed their wedding and the preceding days of preparation. However, Vicki had an uneasy feeling that her husband was in for a degree of disillusionment; she would just have to do what she could to lessen it. It would be a pity to shatter the fantasies about large family life cherished by a lonely little boy all those years ago.

"Well, since we've sorted that one out to everyone's satisfaction but mine," Victoria declared in a tone much more cheerful than her words, "why don't we get out of this crush and go have a civilized dinner somewhere? Dan and Boris won't be able to come until the gallery is empty, but I'll see if I can extricate Bev."

The suggestion was received with both enthusiasm and relief. Max followed her into the office when she went to collect her coat, closing the door quietly but decisively on the noise outside.

"Oh, dear," Vicki murmured, shrugging herself out of his jacket. "You're cross." It was a statement, not a question.

"Are you surprised?" Max took his coat and ran a swift, checking eye over the contents.

"Well, I'd meant to tell you what I wanted to do, but things happened a bit fast," Vicki explained apologetically.

"Look, quite apart from the fact that I totally disapprove of manufacturing excuses to avoid social obligations, I do not care to be implicated in your dubious schemes without my consent." Max regarded her gravely. Vicki began to feel thoroughly discomfited, and fought the ludicrous urge to drop her eyes and shuffle her feet.

"I am suitably chastened," she said with a slight smile. "Can we talk about something else now? I won't do it again."

Max shook his head at her in that special way he had—expressing both amusement and resigned acceptance. "You're utterly incorrigible, Victoria Randall. Of course you'll do it again! Just don't expect me to back you up."

"Not in that, maybe," Vicki said slowly, "but there are going to be times . . ."

"My darling, do you think I would sit back and allow anyone, even your mother, to make your life uncomfortable?" Max took the slim shoulders beneath the white silk shirt and gave her a slight, reassuring shake. "I think I've got the picture, Victoria—I'm not generally considered to be obtuse."

"Now you're making me laugh, Max." Her eyes were slightly misty as she looked up at him. "Who could ever suggest such a thing? You're the most perceptive, understanding—"

She got no further as his mouth demanded and then enforced her silence.

"And you, my love, are a genius." Max drew back a fraction, just enough to allow him to speak. "Not just with your brush on canvas, but with your brush on the world . . . and I adore you."

❦ 12 ❦

"Hey, what are you doing over there?" Max's soft voice penetrated the velvety darkness of the night as he reached for the tightly curled ball lying at the farthest extremity of the wide bed. He pulled her across the cold space between them, and Vicki settled against him with a small sigh.

"I've always slept like that in this bed," she murmured,

"ever since I was first put in it at the age of about five. It always seemed so huge and cold, somehow." She chuckled reminiscently. "Tom used to be petrified I'd fall out, but when he told Mother I ought to have a bed more suitable to my size, she just said vaguely that I'd grow into it."

Max curled himself around her. "What an odd thing to say."

"Wasn't it?" Vicki agreed. "But Tom put a line of pillows down the middle and that made it much better—but I still slept on the edge."

"Poor little mite—what a pathetic story."

"They run in families," Vicki said, with a slight smile in the darkness.

"I suppose they do," Max murmured, trying to rearrange her limbs to fit the curve of his body. "Darling, whatever's the matter? You're usually so soft and cuddly, but now you're all bones and angles!"

"I'm sorry." Vicki made an effort to relax. "It's just that it feels strange, somehow, being in this bed, in this room, with you. We've never slept together here before."

"Is that why you insisted on wearing this ridiculous nightgown?" His hands pulled it up to her waist as he rolled her on top of him, maneuvering the cotton garment up her body and over her head, drawing the sleeves off her arms and tossing the offending article to the floor. "That's much better." He sighed with satisfaction. "Now I can feel you properly."

Vicki lay still and contented against his length as he stroked her body. "I think I'm being a bit silly, don't you?" she muttered into the hollow of his neck.

"Not necessarily," he reassured. "You can't deny your

past experiences, particularly with such vivid memories." He patted her bottom with friendly comfort, and Vicki burrowed against him.

"It's so odd," she tried to explain, "but when I come home I seem to regress somehow, go back to being the child of the household. Father treats me with his usual absentminded affection, and Mother persists in behaving as if I'm still her recalcitrant daughter."

"So you are," Max chuckled.

"Not recalcitrant," Vicki protested.

"By Isobel's standards, you are—and always will be."

"But I made a good marriage," she teased, her teeth nipping the skin of his shoulder. "That should have made everything all right . . . Ow! No, don't, please, Max!" Her body convulsed as she squealed in protest under his tickling fingers.

"Apologize!" Max demanded, laughter quivering in his voice as he rolled her beneath him and held her wriggling body firmly with one hand while the other continued implacably to exact the penalty.

The thought flashed through Vicki's mind, even as she struggled, that a few months ago her teasing remark might well have resulted in quite another reaction. "I'm sorry . . . truly, I am," she gasped desperately. "Oh, you're so horrid! It's the middle of the night."

"Horrid, am I?" he growled, sliding his hands beneath her hips, raising her to meet him as he became a part of her. "Let me show you just how horrid I can be!"

Vicki relaxed with a deep sigh, but only momentarily as Max increased the speed of his movements, driving deeply, relentlessly within her, bringing her to a near-febrile pitch of excitement and passion as she reached for him, her own movements matching the urgent thrusts, her hands clawing his back as her heels, pressed against his buttocks, told him of her own urgency. The blood roared in her ears as the volcano erupted in a seemingly endless series of shattering explosions, and their joyous cries of completion rang heedlessly through the darkness.

It seemed an eternity before her pulses slowed and her racing blood assumed something approximating its normal sedate course through her veins. "Sweet heaven, my love," Vicki whispered. "What was that? Were you trying to drive out demons?"

"Sort of," he mumbled from his own plane of satisfied exhaustion. "Did I succeed?"

"And how!" She laughed weakly. "All the ghosts are banished to outer darkness, now that I've truly consummated my girlhood bed!" A fit of utterly exhausted giggles overtook her. "We've probably awakened the entire household!"

"Hush," Max whispered, burying her head against his chest in an effort to smother her laughter, although his own was every bit as uncontrolled. "If we didn't, we certainly will in a minute. Oh, *do* control yourself!"

"I ca . . . can't," Vicki gasped helplessly, struggling feebly in his hold. "You're suffocating me."

"Well, stop it then—you're making us both hysterical!" Max tightened his grasp, fighting to control his own hilarity as he held her still until her body had stopped shaking and the continuing giggles were at least muted.

"Oh, dear," Vicki sighed, molding herself against him with a body no longer all bones and angles but rather resembling a perfectly malleable ball of putty. "I do love you—

you're so *good* for me."

"That makes me feel like a mound of unappetizing spinach," Max grumbled, and then realized his mistake. "Oh, don't start again, Victoria, please," he begged. "We must get some sleep."

"I'm trying," she groaned. "Let me up and I'll see if a trip to the bathroom in this freezing house will sober me up."

Max released her and she stumbled across the darkened room, still bent double with laughter. But the cold night air on her bare, overheated skin did its work, and it was a quiet, sober, shivering figure who leaped back under the heavy feather quilt to snuggle against his warmth.

An imperative thump at the wooden door brought Vicki swimming upward from the green depths of far too short a sleep.

"Vicki! You awake in there? We're leaving in a half-hour." It was Tom's voice, sounding appallingly bright, cheerful, and alert.

"Oh, help!" Vicki groaned. "It's Thanksgiving morning, isn't it?"

Max struggled upright, sleepily running his hands through his hair so that it stood up in a soft halo around his head. Before he could say anything, however, there was another imperious knock.

"Vicki—better hurry," Tom yelled again. "You know what happens to lazy little sisters!" Laughter bubbled in the cheerful voice.

"Not when they're married!" Victoria yelled back. "But I'm coming—okay?"

"Breakfast in ten minutes, then." The sound of retreating

footsteps down the hall outside brought a temporary peace.

"What *does* happen to lazy little sisters?" Max inquired with interest, looking at his wife's exasperated yet resigned expression.

"They get dumped in a tub of cold water," Vicki said succinctly, dragging herself out of the warm bed with a yawn and the most obvious reluctance.

"What a good idea," Max observed. "I wonder why I never thought of that."

"Probably because, fortunately for us both, I don't happen to be your sister," Vicki retorted. "Now get up!"

"Would you mind telling me what the hell's going on around here?" he asked pleasantly. "It's only six-thirty."

"You are about to be introduced to a sacred, long-standing Carrolton ritual," Vicki informed him. "A ten-mile hike through the hills—the four of us have done it every Thanksgiving since I can remember. It's all right once you start— it's just this bit that's so horrendous."

Max frowned and she caught a flash of hesitancy in his blue eyes. "I'll just stay here, darling, and charm your mother and the aunts," he said quietly.

Vicki realized instantly what he was thinking—he didn't want to intrude on a purely family tradition. He was so incredibly sensitive! With a sudden movement, she dragged the covers off him. "Get out of that bed, Max Randall, you're not ducking out of this one. If you think I'm taking one step outside this house without you, you can think again! And if I refuse to go, *you'll* be responsible for the biggest family row since the Creation."

"For such a little thing, you can be so incredibly fierce." Max smiled softly and Vicki smiled back—there was no need for explanation; they understood each other completely. He drew her against him, just as another imperious knock shook the door. "Oh, Lord!" Max groaned. "What now? Hello?" he called.

"Can I come in? I've brought you some tea," Tom responded blithely.

"No, you can't, Tom!" Max exclaimed. "Just leave it outside the door, thanks."

There was a short pause and then Tom's voice again, this time much more subdued. "Sorry—didn't mean to catch you at an awkward moment."

"Oh, Tom, *do* go away," Vicki begged on a choke of laughter. "We'll be down in a minute."

"Yes . . . well, see you then," Tom muttered, and beat a hasty retreat.

"I did warn you." Vicki grinned. "No one in this family is a respecter of persons, and my marital status makes absolutely no difference to anything."

Max glanced down his naked length and pronounced ruefully, "That little interruption certainly appears to have cooled my ardor."

Vicki chortled and reached with intimate fingers. "I could soon do something about that, but we don't have the time right now, my love."

"Guess not." Max sighed and disappeared into the bathroom. Vicki followed him, splashing cold water on her face with a shudder, brushing her teeth vigorously, ducking beneath Max's arm as he ran the shaver over his long jaw as he stared intently into the mirror above the basin.

"You don't need to look beautiful for this exercise." Vicki swatted him playfully on her way back to the bedroom.

"You're only going to end up pouring sweat and covered in mud!"

Max came after her, laughing, but Vicki leaped agilely out of his reach, dancing across the bed. "Can't catch me!"

"That's what you think." He grinned. "Unfortunately, we don't have time for what would then ensue."

"Excuses, excuses," she taunted, dragging on her clothes hastily and keeping a wary eye on him.

Max chuckled but turned to his own dressing. "No, don't put that on," he said suddenly, seeing her about to pull a heavy sweater over her head. "I was going to give you this later, but this seems an appropriate moment." He pulled a tissue-wrapped package out of a drawer.

Vicki shook her head at him. "Another present, Max?"

"Close your eyes and lift up your arms," he instructed cheerfully, ignoring her question.

Vicki did so and felt something thick, heavy, and incredibly warm slide over her head as her arms were manipulated into the sleeves. "Can I look?" She felt him pull whatever it was firmly over her hips, patting it into shape as he turned her around.

"Go ahead." He sounded utterly satisfied, and she saw why when she examined herself in the mirror. The blended colors of the thick Norwegian sweater were those of her eyes and hair, and the slim column of her neck rose from a wide, deep green roll neck.

"It's gorgeous," Vicki said without surprise. "I don't know how you do it—I'm almost never with you when you shop, but you *never* make a mistake."

"That's because you *are* always with me." Max stood behind her, his hands cupping the small mounds of her breasts beneath the wool. "There's never been a moment, since I first saw you, when you haven't been with me."

Vicki leaned back against his strong frame, resting her head on his shoulder, smiling at him in the mirror. "Since you're always with me, even when I'm working, that seems both inevitable and utterly logical, my darling."

"Yes, it does, doesn't it?" Max declared with an air of smug satisfaction that brought a gurgle of laughter to her throat.

"Come on, we'd better go downstairs." Reluctantly, she straightened, running a gentle caress over his face as she did so. "Oh, Lord," Vicki exclaimed suddenly. "You realize we forgot all about the tea—it'll be stone cold by now. We'd better pour it down the sink, otherwise Tom will be hurt." Opening the door softly, she grabbed the two cups of tepid liquid with a grimace. "I wish they'd remember that I'm the one member of this family who prefers coffee in the morning."

The large kitchen in this sprawling house nestled in the hilly Massachusetts countryside was warm and busy. The three Carrolton brothers seemed to fill any room, however big, Max reflected, bending to greet Milady as she jumped ecstatically at his feet. The rest of the household seemed still to be in their beds—not even a child was around, and there were enough of them in residence this holiday weekend.

"Ah, there you are—the oatmeal's ready." Steve smiled in greeting from the heavy aluminum pot on the stove that he was stirring with great concentration.

"Oh, no," Vicki groaned. "Can't we just settle for a piece of toast?"

"Eat!" Steve placed a large ceramic bowl in front of her

as she slid over the long bench at the pine table. "You can't go out on the hills—"

"With low blood sugar," she finished for him on a resigned note, examining the contents of the bowl. "You'll have to take some of this out, Steve. I refuse to eat it all—I won't be able to move a step with a ton of bricks in my stomach!"

"Eat what you can and leave what you can't," her brother rejoined cheerfully. "Max, you want some of my speciality?"

"He's having it, whether he wants to or not," Vicki declared. "No member of the family's exempt."

Max squeezed her thigh as he swung himself over the bench to sit beside her. He regarded the thick contents of his own bowl with some misgiving, and Vicki grinned.

"It's not *too* bad if you put plenty of brown sugar on it—like so." She suited her actions to the words. "Now, you make a big hole in the middle with the back of a spoon and fill it with cream—like this. Then you just stir it all up. Looks pretty, doesn't it?" Her eyes twinkled merrily, and he burst out laughing.

"I'm convinced!"

"Resigned is more like it," Vicki said, resting her head against his arm for a second.

"Vicki, when did you last clean your boots?" Mike appeared from the laundry room off the kitchen holding a pair of hiking boots at arm's length in front of him.

She shrugged. "No idea. Years ago, I guess. What's the point? They only get muddy again."

"You *cannot* mistreat good equipment!" Mike remonstrated. "I've been telling you that for years."

"Yes. I know you have," Vicki said very quietly. "And I've been trying to tell *you* that what I do with my boots or anything else, for that matter, is entirely *my* business."

A tense silence descended on the room, during which Max stoically consumed his oatmeal. He appeared unconcerned, but every muscle in his face had tensed as he waited for the next installment in what was clearly a familiar argument. He was reluctant to intervene in something that didn't really concern him, but neither was he prepared to allow his wife to be browbeaten by anyone—family or no. Not that she would be. He grinned to himself. Victoria was more than capable of holding her own.

Vicki and Mike continued to look at each other steadily across the room.

"Oh, cool it, the pair of you!" It was Tom who broke the deadlock. "You're both right, and you know it. There's no point squabbling over something this trivial. If Vicki wants to slip and slide in boots caked with three years' worth of mud, that's her affair."

"Thank you, Tom." Vicki smiled sweetly and pushed her half-finished bowl of cereal away from her.

"I wish I knew where we went wrong," Mike muttered very audibly, turning back to the laundry room.

"Why, you pompous . . ." Vicki jumped off the bench and skidded on stockinged feet across the wood floor toward him.

Mike swung around, dropping the boots to catch her up as she hurled herself at him. "Thought that would get you." He chuckled, and she burst into a peal of laughter.

Max sighed and absently exchanged his empty bowl for Vicki's half-full, rejected one—it was really quite palatable.

One of these days he'd be able to operate in the Carrolton way, he supposed, although it obviously took years of practice! He pushed the gloomy thought aside. It was always possible, of course, that his wife enjoyed the contrast.

"Sorry about that," Vicki whispered into his ear as she came up behind him and hugged him. "I know it's not what you're used to."

"I'm learning," Max whispered back, and then pulled her onto his lap with a chuckle. "I hate to say it, my love, but I'm in Mike's corner on this one—mud-caked boots are not only inefficient, they're also potentially dangerous! I'll go clean them for you."

"No." Vicki shook her head vigorously. "I'll do it myself. I clean up my own messes, love."

"But I'd like to," Max said simply.

Vicki smiled softly and kissed him. "I'd hate to interfere with your pleasure, husband." With loving, understanding eyes, she watched him leave the room and then began to set the kitchen to rights. They'd be out all morning, and it was hardly fair to leave the place in a state of chaos with all the culinary preparations that would be going on.

"Let's get this show on the road." Tom tugged on a stray tendril of her hair as she scrubbed the last scraps of oatmeal from the saucepan. "Unless, of course, you'd rather stay here and be domestic," he teased.

"I'm quite happy to do that," Vicki said thoughtfully. "I always feel a bit guilty leaving everything to everyone else."

"Oh, don't be absurd, infant!" Steve broke in, hunching into his jacket. "No one else would want to come, anyway, and you arrived yesterday loaded with pies and cranberry sauce and heaven knows what else! Anyway, most of it's done already—Mother hardly spends her time slaving single-handedly over a hot stove! She's been running a cook and three pairs of helping hands ragged in the last week."

"I don't have a leg to stand on," Vicki admitted cheerfully, knowing that they were right. She dried her hands vigorously and went into the laundry room.

Max handed over her boots. "They were an utter disgrace, Victoria!"

She made a face at him and dropped onto a bench to pull them on. "Who asked you to do them?" It was the way she would have responded to a similar remark from one of her brothers, but she saw the flash—half-surprise, half-annoyance—in his eyes. Fortunately, it was almost immediately replaced by a spark of laughter answering her own.

"I can't think where your brothers went wrong!" Max observed equably.

"I love you," Vicki whispered, her eyes shining with an all-encompassing love.

"And I love you, green eyes, to distraction," Max responded softly.

It was no gentle stroll that they took through a series of steep hills. Max was fascinated, as he always was, by the effortless ease with which his diminutive wife kept up with the long, rolling strides of her brothers. Vicki reached for his hand once or twice. Every now and then, she was conscious that Max was mentally slipping out of the intimate group, observing them as an outsider. The need to reassure him that, although that was fine if it was what he wanted, he belonged to her and she to him, was overpowering.

Her brothers' wives had had their problems with this unusual sibling closeness—they were all a lot older than herself, but even as a child Vicki had been aware of the pangs of puzzled jealousy that her brothers' absolute involvement in her life had caused. It had been one of the contributing factors in her decision to break free at the age of twenty, when she had fought them all in a devastating battle that had rocked the family structure to its very foundations. It had been the right decision for all of them—a fact now openly acknowledged by all except Isobel. That thought brought a slight frown between Vicki's fine eyebrows.

"What's up?" Max, with his ever-observant eye, caught the movement and squeezed her hand.

"Just musing." Vicki smiled. "Isn't this beautiful?" Stopping, she looked around at the snow-covered landscape, trees standing stark and bare against the gray, early-morning sky.

"Utterly," Max responded, accepting, but with reluctance, her evasion of his question.

"Come on, you two! We haven't got all day!" Mike called over his shoulder.

"Bullies, aren't they?" Vicki laughed and, tugging on his hand, set off again, pulling Max beside her.

They returned in a state of merry, muddied fatigue to a kitchen buzzing with life and redolent with the most delicious aromas.

"Home come the hunters," Isobel Carrolton trilled, turning from the stove, looking impossibly elegant in spite of the enormous apron swathed around her slight figure.

"Well, we didn't exactly bring home a brace of pheasants

and a boar," Vicki announced, kissing her mother. "You smell good."

"You, Vicki, need a bath," her mother declared, examining her critically. "But that's a lovely sweater."

"Max gave it to me." Deciding not to respond to provocation, Vicki dipped her fingers into a pan of simmering creamed onions and was rewarded with a sharp tap on the wrist. She grinned cheerfully at her sister-in-law. "Sorry, Liz, but I can't resist them, and I did peel the onions last night."

"You're an incorrigible picker," Liz replied with a chortle, then lifted her face to Steve's kiss. "The apple juice is warming, if you're going to continue tradition with your rum thing."

"Angel wife." Steve laughed, giving her an affectionate pat. "Where are the cinnamon sticks?"

"In the usual place," Isobel answered plaintively. "It really doesn't seem reasonable that you should all return after a morning in the hills and then take over the kitchen when we've all got so much to do. We're going to be thirty for dinner, after all."

Vicki bit her tongue and took the promised ten deep breaths, catching Tom's eye.

"Mother, you say the same thing every year, and we know you don't mean a word of it." He laughed and kissed Isobel warmly.

"You all need baths," she declared severely. "You look just like a litter of puppies. Max, you will make sure Vicki wears something suitable, won't you?"

"You didn't hear that," Max hissed in his wife's ear, "and neither did I. Go take a bath before she says anything else."

Vicki whisked herself out of the kitchen and found, to her amazement, that she was laughing. Isobel would never change—it wasn't that she didn't love her family, but she simply couldn't let go. The only way to deal with it was to ignore it.

Vicki watched the tub fill, stripping off her muddy jeans and socks, pulling the sweater over her head. It was silly to think she alone suffered during the Thanksgiving ritual; they were all involved, including Max now—and he seemed more than capable of dealing with the situation. But then, cantankerous relatives were his speciality. Vicki chuckled to herself.

"I don't know what Steve did with this, but it sure as hell isn't pure apple juice!" Max appeared in the door, two steaming, aromatic mugs on a tray balanced on the flat of his hand. "Aren't you in that bath yet?"

"I am now." Vicki dived for the tub, sinking into the water. "We'll have to share this one. I've overfilled it and there won't be enough hot water for the others."

"Well, shift your backside then," Max demanded cheerfully, handing her a mug and stripping off his clothes with rapid fingers. He slid in facing her, took a deep sip from his cup and gave a sigh of utter pleasure. "What a way to live!"

"Up to a point," Vicki murmured lazily, running her foot up his leg, her toes curling and stroking as if they had a life of their own. "So long as it's only temporary."

"Come on, love, you can handle it." Max stroked her foot but made no effort to move it from its resting place.

"With you around, I can," Vicki told him, smiling softly as his maleness flickered against her caressing toes. "It seems singularly unimportant and irrelevant when I'm with you, and I guess Mother can't help it. I must say, though," she added thoughtfully, "Father would have done everyone a favor if he'd tried to put a stop to it once or twice instead of indulging her all the time. That was what Grandfather used to say, anyway." Vicki laughed in fond reminiscence. "Not that he could do anything, either!"

"Well, you're not going to be like that with your daughter," Max pronounced with conviction.

"Or my sons?"

"Whichever." Leaning forward, he took her elbows and drew her toward him. "Soon, Victoria?" He began to play with her breasts, flicking their crowns with a light fingertip, smiling with satisfaction as they rose beneath his playful touch.

"Whenever you want, my darling." Her arms slipped around his neck as she pressed herself against him, raising herself slightly as he sheathed himself within her beneath the warm benediction of the water. They loved slowly, languorously, reaching a peace of friendship and union that expressed what words alone never could. They had, at last, learned to be married, Vicki thought as her mouth joined with Max's and their wet, satisfied bodies fused in blissful harmony.

❦ 13 ❦

"That's not the time? It can't be!" Vicki gazed in horror at the clock in Dan's office. "I forgot all about the Japanese— at least, no I didn't—oh, Lord!" She began to run distractedly around the room gathering up her possessions. For the last three weeks she'd been reminding herself, "December seventh, December seventh," and now that the day had come . . .

"What on earth are you burbling about?" Dan asked, watching her gyrations with considerable amusement. "What Japanese?"

"Oh, it's a trade delegation," Vicki explained. "Max is having a cocktail party for them at the apartment this evening, and I *have* to be there, but it's supposed to start in five minutes, and look at me!" She gestured vaguely at her jeans and sweater. "I'll have to call Max." She grabbed the phone and then replaced it. "No, Bev, do me a favor, love, and call him—tell him I'm on my way. You're always so diplomatic."

Bev grinned. "What shall I tell him kept you?"

"Oh, anything—he won't believe any excuses, anyway. He knows me too damn well!" Vicki replied unhappily. How could she have done such a thing?

Bev picked up the phone and dialed while Vicki hovered in the door, wasting precious minutes, she knew, but she had to find out Max's reaction—she couldn't face him unprepared.

Bev's soft voice filled the room, her large brown eyes glowing with amusement. After a minute, she covered the receiver with one hand and turned to Vicki. "He wants to speak to you."

"But I'm supposed to be on my way," Vicki wailed in an undertone.

Bev raised her eyebrows. "You did just say he knows you too well." She held out the phone and Vicki took it reluctantly.

"Max?"

"I'm sending Ed to pick you up." Max's voice fell crisply on her ear. "You'll never get a cab at this time of day, and it's raining cats and dogs—you'll get soaked if you walk."

"Look, darling, I'm—"

"I'll hear it later, Victoria," he interrupted. "Wait downstairs—Ed will be there in five minutes." The line went dead and Vicki replaced the phone with a slight shrug.

"Well, I'll see you all soon—if I come out of this one intact!" she added miserably. "I remembered when I came in here and then . . . oh, I don't know—sometimes I think Max and I live on two totally different planets. Bye now." Shaking her head in disbelief, she ran downstairs to wait just inside the shelter of the door.

Ed appeared within minutes of her arrival and whisked her through the crowded streets with a speed and skill that seemed to ignore the very existence of the frenetic traffic. He opened the door for her as they drew up outside the apartment building, and with a mumbled word of thanks, Vicki darted through the downpour and into the warmth of the lobby, managing a brief acknowledgment of the doorman's greeting as she hurled herself into the elevator. She had barely gotten her key into the lock of the front door when it swung open. Max stood looking down at her.

"Oh, dear, darling . . ." She struggled for an explanation and gave up. "Are you *very* mad?" She gazed up at him, a picture of anxious wistfulness.

"Livid," he responded coolly, and then, to her unutterable relief, his face split in a broad grin. "Impossible woman! Hello." Tilting her chin with a long finger, he kissed the corner of her mouth. "That's not actually what you deserve, you know."

"I know." Vicki smiled. "I'm very sorry."

"So you should be—now hurry up and get changed." Vicki blew him a kiss and headed for the bedroom, catching a quick glimpse of the bustle in the living room as the caterers prepared for the party. Emerging, wrapped in a towel, from a very hasty shower, she found Max in the bedroom going through her closet. He crooked an imperative finger, and she crossed the room with a slight smile.

"Let's have a look at you." But then, instead of lifting her face for his usual, intense scrutiny, Max calmly pulled the towel away from her and ran a long, slow, smoldering look down her body.

"Max," Vicki whispered as her nipples hardened, her skin tingling. "Don't do that. We don't have time."

"I can look at you if I want," he replied smoothly. "Anyway, we have a half-hour."

"We have *what!*" Vicki gazed at him as a sudden surge of annoyance chased away her remorse. "Are you telling me you deliberately gave me a time earlier than the real one?"

Max laughed. "My darling, I haven't lived with you all this time without learning to take some elementary precautions. I always ensure that you have plenty of leeway if I'm not around to supervise your every move!"

"Well!" Vicki stood, hands on hips, glaring at her husband's laughing face, for a moment speechless. Then, suddenly, the humor of the situation hit her, and she grinned appreciatively. "If you knew what a state I've been in, Max Randall . . ."

"You earned every minute of it." He chuckled. "Supposing it *had* been the right time?"

"I guess." Vicki shrugged acceptingly. "But you do

realize since I now know your little secret, it won't work anymore?"

"Oh, yes, it will," Max said confidently. "I'm not necessarily predictable—sometimes it will be the right time and sometimes it won't. And you won't know which until you arrive."

"You are utterly abominable!" Vicki declared with a choke of laughter. "But very clever. Now, let me get dressed, otherwise we really shall be late."

"Mr. Randall?" Josefa, who had been transplanted from Westchester for the occasion, spoke softly from outside the door.

"Yes, Josefa?" Max turned toward the voice.

"I'm sorry to disturb you, but I need to know how you want the food served. I would ask Mrs. Randall, but . . ."

"I'll be right out, Josefa." Max chuckled at the housekeeper's apologetic tone. "Wear the Indian silk," he instructed Victoria briskly, striding toward the door. "And the Egyptian necklace," he added as an afterthought, grinning cheerfully at her indignant expression.

Vicki put her tongue out at him, her green eyes sparkling. "You're getting controlling again, husband."

"With cause," he responded smoothly, and left the room.

Deciding ruefully that he had a point, Vicki dressed rapidly, emerging into the living room just as the doorbell rang. "You look positively edible," Max whispered as they turned as one to greet their first guests.

It was a highly successful evening, largely, Max decided, due to Victoria's ability to smooth out any awkward situation. It was not the easiest party, with their Japanese guests coming from a quite different culture and with many of them speaking little English. It didn't appear to matter, though; Victoria seemed able to communicate regardless. It was quite clear that she was enjoying herself as much as her guests were, but then, her years of travel had given her an innate appreciation and understanding of cultural differences. She might be chaotic and tempestuous on occasion, Max reflected with a warm, inner smile of love, but she was utterly reliable in any area where it truly mattered, and he couldn't begin to conceive of a situation where she might let him down.

Rain drummed ceaselessly, relentlessly, against the long windows of the living room. It was the following Saturday, late in the afternoon of what had been a blissfully relaxing day. Max leaned over and threw another log on the crackling fire, then glanced at his wife, curled barefoot in an enormous wing chair beside the hearth, her bright head bent over her sketch pad.

"Darling?"

Vicki looked up and frowned. "Hold still a second, there's something about your eyebrows that I keep missing."

Max obligingly remained still until she nodded, satisfied. "Sorry, you were saying?" Vicki stuck her pencil in her mouth and raised an inquiring eyebrow.

"I was wondering if you'd found a studio in the city yet. I want to move in immediately after the New Year—it doesn't give us much time."

Vicki's heart sank. Oh, well, it had to come sometime, she'd just been putting off the inevitable. "Look, love, I'm not going to be able to move until I've finished what I'm working on at the moment." It was his birthday present, but she wasn't about to tell him that.

"What on earth do you mean? You're not going to be able to? We agreed that it *has* to be." His tone was perfectly calm, as if this was some minor point of disagreement to which the answer was obvious. But it wasn't.

"I need the light in the studio," she explained patiently, wondering why her heart was thudding and her palms suddenly damp and clammy.

"You can find somewhere as good," Max said, still calm, still certain.

"No, I can't. At least, certainly not for this work. I started it in a certain light, and I can't possibly continue it in a different one. No two places are the same—there's no way I can find anything even approximating what I have upstairs."

"Well, why the hell did you start it in the first place, then?" he inquired. A note of exasperation had crept into his voice, although it was still no more than that. "You knew when we would be moving."

Because your birthday's at the end of January, Vicki thought fiercely. But she said, simply, "I never know how long something will take, love. It would have made no difference, whatever I'd started."

"Then you should have waited until we moved," Max told her bluntly. "You'll just have to put it on one side until we come back in April. You can always start something else in the new place."

Vicki seemed to be enclosed in an icy fog. He was telling her that her work was of secondary importance in their joint lives, and he was telling her that as if it were an indisputable fact that she should have known all along. A powerful anger was rising inside her, and she fought it down desperately. She just had to tell him quietly and calmly that he was wrong. She had worked out a perfectly adequate compromise in preparation for this inevitable confrontation, and Max was going to have to accept it.

"It doesn't work like that, Max," she began, but got no further.

"What are you trying to say, Victoria? You know damn well I can't risk being snowbound out here in the sticks during the winter. I *must* be able to get into the office at all times, and quickly! No, let me finish," he ordered sharply, seeing her mouth open to interrupt. "You also know that we have a host of social engagements during those months, utterly vital engagements that we can't afford to miss. How can you possibly commute back and forth at night in the weather conditions you know we're going to get! You can't even arrive on time when you're already in the city—as we discovered last week! It's neither logical nor realistic!"

"Neither logical nor realistic for *you,* perhaps," Vicki said, keeping her voice low and even with a supreme effort. "Those engagements are only really necessary for *you . . .*"

"What!" Max exploded, leaping to his feet with such suddenness that Vicki cowered involuntarily in her chair. "I don't know what it is you're getting at, Victoria, but I don't like it one little bit!"

"I have a reasonable suggestion." Vicki stood up; it didn't give her much advantage, but it was better than shrinking against the back of the chair while this furious individual towered over her.

"There are *no* reasonable suggestions," Max stated flatly, making a visible effort to calm himself. "We move on January second, and that's final."

"Don't you dare tell me what's final and what isn't!" Vicki gave up the attempt to hold her anger in check. "I am *not* moving until I finish the painting. You can live in the apartment, and I'll come in any evening you need me, weather permitting, and you can come here on weekends."

The face above hers went deathly white, the blue eyes narrowed into chips of cold quartz. "I don't believe what you just said." Max's voice was a low growl. "You are calmly suggesting a part-time marriage as a reasonable compromise? Look, Victoria, you are my wife, whether you like it or not; there is no place in my conception of marriage for this modern fad for commuting partnerships!" He spat the phrase with utter disdain.

"Why you archaic, chauvinistic, self-centered . . ." Vicki stopped in midsentence as, to her shocked horror, Max shook her—clearly not as hard as he wanted to, but it was enough.

"How dare you?" With a choked sob, she tore herself out of his hold and ran blindly from the room and out of the house, heedless of the rain and her shoeless state.

The slam of the front door shivered through Max's motionless figure. He turned and, with shaking hands, poured himself a tumbler of bourbon from the decanter and drained it in two gulps. How the hell could she have made such a suggestion? She was his wife, for godsake! But she had warned him often enough in the past about her feelings toward marriage—he should have listened.

Vicki ran through the soaked grass, through the dripping trees, then pushed through the prickly hedge at the bottom and out into the lane. She ran without motive and heedless of her direction. She was running simply from the emotional devastation of the last hour. How could he have said those things, made those assumptions, touched her in that way? And she had actually believed that they now understood about marriage—why, they understood nothing! Nothing about each other, nothing about marriage. But she *had* been willing to compromise—Max hadn't been prepared to yield an inch! His ideas and his life came first and would admit of *no* compromise.

It was pitch-dark now, and as the desperate, adrenaline-produced energy died, Vicki slowed, realizing at the same instant that her feet were in agony. She limped to the grass verge, bent double, gasping for breath. She had no idea where she was, only that she was frozen, drenched, and alone in a black, murky country lane. There were no comforting lights indicating human habitation—the houses were all set well back from the road and up long driveways, hidden behind the privacy of bordering trees. But she was going to have to find one and knock on a door. The thought of the image she must present sent a shudder of misery through her slight frame—she'd be lucky if anyone let her in, but there was no alternative. Why did she never think about consequences before yielding to impulse? Wearily, Vicki trudged along the grass verge, every step an excruciating effort.

Max was on his second bourbon before some realization of the time hit him. Vicki had been out for over an hour. The rain lashed against the window and, with a muttered exclamation, he set down the glass and ran for his car keys.

The car lights swooped down the lane, illuminating the small figure. Vicki paused, her heart pounding uncomfortably. She presented a perfect target for anyone with malevolent intent, but it was also possible that the car's driver might be curious enough at the strange sight of a lone woman tramping up the lane in a monsoon to stop and offer rescue. The car passed her, its sleek lines unmistakable, and pulled onto the verge a few yards ahead. The passenger door opened, barring further progress.

"Get in." His voice was clipped and flat.

Vicki climbed into the car without a word, huddling into the bucket seat, her feet now screaming their complaint at the abuse she had inflicted on them. Max leaned over and fastened her seat belt in silence, reaching for the door that she was too exhausted to close for herself. The door slammed, enclosing them in warm, wordless darkness. Vicki began to shiver uncontrollably, and Max swore as he put the Porsche in gear.

The lights of the house penetrated her miserable reverie much sooner than Vicki had expected. Surprisingly, she had covered much less ground than she thought during her impetuous flight. The garage doors opened as Max pressed the signal button on the dash and they drove into the light. Still in silence, he cut the engine, pressed the release button on her seat belt, and came around to her side of the car, opening the door. Vicki scrambled out and couldn't prevent the gasp of pain as her injured feet hit the hard concrete.

Max glanced down at the floor and gazed in horror at the bloodstained footprint. "Dear Lord, Victoria! What have you done to yourself?" Sweeping her drenched body into his arms, he ran with her through the rain to the front door, resting her on an upraised knee, cradled against his chest, as he unlocked it.

"You're too wet to put on the bed," he muttered when they reached the bedroom. He strode with her into the bathroom, setting her on a cork-topped stool by the basin while he filled the tub. "Get undressed. I'm going downstairs to find the antiseptic."

Vicki struggled with her clothes, but her hands seemed unable to obey the message from her brain. She was lost in the sodden wool of her sweater when Max reappeared with a large tumbler of rich golden liquid and a bottle of antiseptic.

"Oh, hell!" He was more alarmed than he was prepared to admit even to himself as he dragged the sweater over her head, stripped off the remainder of her clothes, and put her shivering, shaking body into the tub. Vicki cried out as the hot water stung her feet and fought the threatening tears with her last reserves of strength.

Max seized a washcloth and began to scrub her cold-reddened skin with a fierce vigor that expressed his fear more clearly than words could have done, but, at last, Vicki stopped shaking. Max handed her the tumbler.

"Drink this—you're going to need some type of anesthetic when I deal with your feet."

Vicki took a gulp of the mellow whiskey and choked as it slid too quickly down her throat. "I can't, Max." She held out the glass to him as he knelt beside the tub, but he shook his head in a curt negative.

"Take it slowly." Lifting one of her feet out of the water, he swore softly. "They're cut to ribbons! What an idiotic thing to do!"

Vicki sighed. She felt much stronger now, although it was quite obvious that Max, in spite of his ministrations, was still furious. In a way, that helped to clear her mind. Her own fury had passed, as it always did, but it was replaced by the calm certainty that Max had been wrong on this occasion, much more so than she had—and he was going to have to come to that realization. It was unfortunate that she had foolishly run out like that, since her present condition did give him the right to be annoyed, but that was a trivial issue compared with its cause.

"Can you stand up?" Max broke the chain of her thoughts and she nodded, getting to her feet. It hurt like the devil, but she wasn't going to admit it. Seeing that she was quite capable, Max left her to dry herself and took her half-empty glass downstairs to refill it. When he returned, she was sitting on the bed in a bathrobe.

"Drink this and then lie on your stomach," he instructed, giving her the glass.

"Max, getting drunk will only make things worse," Vicki protested.

"Oh, do as you're told," he said impatiently.

Anger sparked in her green eyes, but Vicki placed the glass untouched on the night table and stretched prone on the bed. Max sat at the end of the bed and lifted her feet onto his knee. There was total silence for the next ten minutes as he carefully picked out pieces of gravel and grit from the cuts, swabbing them liberally with antiseptic. Only the involuntary clenching of her buttock muscles beneath the robe indicated the pain he knew he was inflicting, but he fought the sick feeling in the pit of his stomach and continued resolutely, until he was satisfied that there were no foreign bodies left to cause infection.

Vicki didn't turn over for a long time after he had finished, and Max stood looking helplessly at her still figure. "Victoria, drink your scotch and get into bed, please." He touched her shoulder and she rolled slowly onto her back, her eyes red and swollen. In spite of his anger, his heart lurched painfully. *Had* he been responsible for this? He maneuvered her under the covers and waited as she finished the contents of the glass and burrowed into the bed.

"Get some sleep," Max said quietly. "I'm not ready to come to bed yet." The door closed quietly, leaving Vicki in darkness and a buzzing haze of misery. But she couldn't think clearly any longer—they would have to sort this one out tomorrow, when they were both calm and could again reach the rock-solid foundations of their love, from where a solution had to be found.

❧ 14 ❧

Vicki awoke to pale wintry sunshine and an empty bed. She knew instantly that Max had not slept beside her—her body told her so as clearly as did the cold neatness of the sheets. For a long time, she lay stiffly as a premonition of disaster filled her, then overwhelmed her. Something had happened to them that she didn't think she could handle. She swung herself to the floor, conscious of the stiffness in her muscles, a nagging, whiskey ache behind her temples, and the soreness of her feet. In the bathroom, she drank two glasses of water, took two aspirins, and examined her feet. They were a bruised mess, but no longer bleeding. What a damn-fool thing to have done! Limping back to the bedroom, Vicki tugged a brush through her tangled curls. Her face, white, heavy-eyed, and smudged, stared back at her from the mirror. Vicki decided that she had never seen herself look such a wreck, and turned with a sigh to make her way downstairs in search of Max.

She found him in his office, unshaven, gray-faced, and hollow-eyed, sitting behind the desk tapping a pen absently on the blotter as he stared sightlessly into space.

"How are your feet?" His eyes focused, reluctantly almost, as he looked at her.

"Not too bad," Vicki said, trying to sound cheerful. "Have you been up all night?"

"Couldn't sleep," Max said shortly.

"Oh." Vicki chewed her lip—this was horrible; she could never have imagined such a cold, dead atmosphere between them. "Would you like coffee?"

"There's some already made. It's in the kitchen," he replied dully. "I'm going to shower and shave."

"Why don't you go to bed for a couple of hours?" Vicki placed a tentative hand on his arm as he passed on his way to the door. He ignored it totally, and a bleak coldness swept through her again.

"I'm not tired, and I have a lot of work to get through today."

"Yes, of course. Shall I make breakfast then?" Her hand dropped uselessly to her side.

"Maybe later—I'm not too hungry right now." Max left the room, and Vicki realized that he had only once looked at her during the entire exchange.

She fixed herself breakfast and ate automatically, recognizing her body's need for food at its present low ebb and her own need for the strength to deal with whatever this horror was. It was some time later when she heard his tread on the stairs, much heavier than the usual light footsteps; she heard him cross the hall, and then the door to his office closed with a curious finality.

Tears pricked behind her eyes as she realized that she had no idea what to do next. She couldn't remember a time when she had been at such a loss. Her instincts weren't always right, but she had never before been so completely devoid of ideas. People didn't behave the way Max was behaving—but then, he had told her Randalls did. With a furrowed brow, Vicki poured two cups of coffee.

Max turned, frowning, from the telex as she came in. He was clean shaven, in casual cord pants and a fawn cashmere sweater over an open-neck blue-checked shirt—his usual neat, orderly, fresh self, except that his face was a blank, the eyes expressionless stones. He looked utterly daunting, and Vicki's resolution faltered, but she wasn't a Carrolton for nothing.

"Max, we have to talk." She put the cups on the desk and faced him squarely.

"Victoria, I am neither able nor willing to talk to you," he said coldly.

"Max, you *have* to. You can't fester with resentment like this." Her hand moved toward him, fluttered, then fell, rejected, as he made no responding gesture.

"I'd rather you kept off your feet today," he told her flatly. "You'll open up the cuts again if you walk around."

"Oh, damn my feet!" Vicki exclaimed. "They're not in the least important. I admit I was stupid, but we have to talk about why that happened."

"There's nothing to discuss," Max said tiredly. "You made your views about this marriage partnership perfectly clear last night—I had somehow forgotten that you had done so very lucidly before we got married, or, at least, I hadn't realized that they hadn't changed."

"Max, you are being *so* unfair!" He was slipping away from her, and she was watching it happen in helpless frustration. "I thought we understood each other. I thought we accepted the need to compromise."

"So did I," Max said simply. "I was wrong."

"Look, love," she made one last, desperate try. "We are totally different people, with different working lives, goals, attitudes, but that doesn't have to mean we can't put them together—each be enriched by the other's. We have so much to offer each other."

"So I thought." Max turned back to the telex. "Oh, thanks for the coffee."

"You're welcome." It took every ounce of self-control to keep from hurling the cup at him, but to do so would merely put her at a disadvantage, and she was disadvantaged enough already! Vicki hobbled back to the kitchen, noticing with irritation that she was leaving bloody footprints again. Damn the man! Why did he always have to be right? Except that he wasn't, this time.

Milady looked up hopefully as Vicki sat down on a chair and began to bathe her feet with antiseptic again. The animal had that bewildered, guilty look that dogs wore when there was anger and tension around them. The St. Bernard's huge head rested heavily on her knee, and Vicki stroked it with a sudden need for comfort, even of the mute, animal variety.

"You'll have to go outside on your own today," she murmured, pulling the long, floppy ears. "I can't take you, and I wouldn't bet on Max."

The ears pricked at the familiar sound of the name. At the same moment, Max came into the kitchen. Milady hurled herself at him, prancing around, yelping joyfully. "All right, old thing, I'll take you for a walk in a minute. Victoria, there's blood all over the hall. Let me look at your feet."

Vicki submitted to the frowning examination only because she had no option. "They need bandaging." Max stood up. "That is, if you insist on walking around all day."

"Well, I can hardly spend the day in bed," Vicki muttered.

"I fail to see why not. You're overdue for a rest as it is." Max reached into a cabinet, found what he was looking for, and with swift, efficient fingers bound up her feet. "I'll take Milady out now."

Vicki remained sitting in the deserted kitchen. As he'd bandaged her feet, Max's hands had been so impersonal— it was almost impossible to imagine that they had ever made love, shared the utter intimacy of bodies and minds, joined in joy and laughter. Her laughing, loving husband had vanished into the icy infinity of the wasteland.

It took three days before Vicki reached the point where she knew she could go on in this way no longer. They continued to share the same bed, but Max never came up until he thought she was asleep and, after the first rejection, she had become adept at pretending that she was sleeping. If he guessed, he gave no sign. He came home at the usual time, but she dreaded the sound of the car almost as much as she dreaded their evening meal, when they exchanged small talk with the impersonal politeness of strangers. Josefa moved silently around the house, clearly aware of what was going on, and once or twice she patted Vicki's hand or squeezed her shoulder in wordless sympathy. It occurred to Vicki that, after all those years with Max's grandfather, this was not an unfamiliar scene for Josefa.

She called Tom, finally, in his office at the end of the day. He heard her out in silence, a silence that continued for an unnervingly long time after she had finished.

"Vicki, you sure you've got this right? Max was really going to insist that you drop everything and follow him?"

"Yes," she said miserably. "I know I reacted irrationally by running out like that, but . . ."

"There was nothing the matter with that," Tom interjected briskly. "Anyone would have done the same—at least, any Carrolton," he added with a short laugh. "Your feet all right now?"

"Yes, fine—just a bit sore . . . but what am I going to do, Tom? He won't talk to me; we haven't touched each other, except accidentally, for four days! It's so . . . so . . . desolate!" Her voice faded, but the quick sniff was not lost on Tom.

"Don't cry, infant. Max just operates differently from the rest of us. He'll come around."

"But when?" she wailed. "I can't work, I can't sleep, I can't do anything in this atmosphere."

"Shall I talk to him?"

"No!" Victoria's tears dried instantly. "I don't need anyone to intercede—I just wanted a second opinion."

"All right, Vicki. Here's your second opinion." The voice was comfortingly brisk and matter-of-fact. "You have two choices, as I see it. Either you wait it out, or you go stay with someone for a couple of days and explain to Max exactly why. He'll have to make his own decision then."

"There's a third choice," Vicki said, almost to herself as her thoughts crystallized.

"Sorry, didn't hear you, Vicki?"

"No, it was nothing, Tom. Thanks for listening, love—and for the second opinion."

"You all right?"

"Much better now." Her voice rang strongly with conviction and she heard his relieved sigh.

"Okay—now you're to call me early tomorrow morning, you hear?"

"I hear." Victoria smiled. "Bye, Tom—and thanks again."

"What are families for? Bye, infant." Vicki replaced the receiver thoughtfully.

When Max came in that evening, she was waiting for him in the hall. "Max, I have something to say."

"Say away." He looked dreadful, Vicki thought; haggard, drawn with lack of sleep, every bit as unhappy as she was. Why then was he incapable of doing anything about it? Taking one small step toward her? But it was up to her, this time.

"We'll move into the apartment on the second of January," Vicki said quietly. It wasn't as much of an effort as she had anticipated—if capitulation was the price of this marriage, then she would pay it. But she had not anticipated Max's response.

"We will not," he stated flatly.

"But . . . but that's what you want," Vicki stammered, once again at a loss.

"But it's not what *you* want. We're staying here." He swung around and strode into the living room.

Vicki stood still for a long moment, and then turned

toward the stairs. Max was going to sacrifice his interests for hers, and she was going to have to pay in blood and tears. He was behaving like a sulky little boy—why couldn't he grow up? But this was a game she was no longer prepared to play. She felt neither anger nor resentment, just calm resolution as she dialed the number of Bonnie's apartment in Greenwich Village.

"Hello?" her friend's cheerful voice answered on the third ring.

"Bonnie, it's Vicki. Can I come stay for a couple of nights?"

"Sure, Vicki. Trouble?" As always, Bonnie went directly to the point.

"Sort of—I don't want to talk about it right now. See you in an hour or so."

"Okay, Vicki. Drive carefully."

"Will do." Vicki replaced the receiver, put a few things into an overnight bag, and went downstairs. Max was looking moodily into the empty fireplace grate as she paused in the living room doorway.

"Max, I'm going to stay with Bonnie for a few days. I can't take this kind of punishment any longer. Think things through, and when you've decided what you want to do, call me. I'll be waiting." She spoke gently but firmly, and without waiting for a response went quickly out of the house, to the car standing in the driveway.

Max stood stunned, and then something exploded in his head with all the force of a double-barreled shotgun. He hurtled out of the house, wrenching open the car door, registering only vaguely Vicki's startled expression as he yanked the keys out of the ignition, ignoring the pained squawk from the engine already in gear.

"You are *not* leaving me, Victoria Randall," Max growled menacingly, seizing her upper arm in a ferocious grip as he dragged her out of the car. He hauled her back to the house and into the fortunately deserted kitchen.

At this point, Vicki was beyond either shock or even simple surprise. She had never been manhandled in this way before and just stood still as he held her, the pure fire of anger at last enlivening those previously dull blue eyes.

"You will *never, ever* run out on me again! Do you understand?"

"I wasn't running out on you," Vicki demurred. "I was giving *you* the opportunity to run." If Max heard her words, they didn't sink in. Releasing her, he began to pace around the kitchen, as his hurt-fueled anger and bewilderment at last found expression in a seemingly endless tirade.

All the pent-up tension slowly floated away from her body as she watched him. This was all right. This she could understand and deal with. Max tore her character to shreds as he stormed around the room. Those years in Europe had turned her into a stubborn, selfish, spoiled brat who lived only for her work! A plate flew across the kitchen and smashed into myriad fragments against the wall.

At least it wasn't one of the Wedgwood plates, Vicki reflected, hoisting herself up onto the counter top, kicking her heels idly against the cabinet door beneath. She had no idea what it meant to live with someone else! Max raged. A second plate joined the first, and Vicki controlled her bubble of laughter.

"There's a filing cabinet in the office," she remarked as Max paused for breath.

"What?" He swung around on her.

"I said, there's a filing cabinet in the office. You might want to go sit on it. I can vouch for its salutary effect on lost tempers."

There was an instant of total silence as Max's face registered a series of emotions with such rapidity that Vicki couldn't catch them all.

"Get off there!" Max strode toward her, lifting her off the counter, holding her away from him as she regarded him with fearless curiosity. "What did you just make me do, Victoria?"

"I didn't make you do anything," she replied calmly. "You did it all yourself. Do you think you could either put me down or hug me?"

He did the latter, crushing her with a fierce, hungry need that almost, but not quite, banished the last four days into outer darkness. "Oh, God, Victoria, I've missed you so." The words rustled against her numbed, bruised lips.

"I've missed *you,* my love. You must never go away from me like that again. I can't deal with it." She was drinking in the scent of his skin with all the desperation of the long-deprived as her body reached against his length in an attempt to become a part of him.

"Never," Max whispered. "I can't deal with it, either." Lifting her easily, he carried her into the living room. "I didn't mean any of those things, my own." He held her, looking with intense, anxious eyes into her face.

"Oh, yes, you did," Vicki smiled, touching his lips with a gentle finger. "You meant every one of those words—and there's a fair amount of truth in them. You know what they say about no smoke without fire."

"Victoria, don't, please!" Max rasped miserably. "Darling, it's quite all right. We're none of us perfect. I have elements of the spoiled brat in me, and so do you. We just have to smooth each other's edges and accept the differences." She smiled with unutterable tenderness as she offered reassurance and reaffirmed her knowledge of their love.

"Will you help me?" Max gazed at her with a total intensity as he asked his question.

"I'll be pacing you every step of the way, my love." She repeated the words he had spoken in Quebec and saw the answering light leap into his eyes as he put her gently on the couch.

"Victoria, my own," Max's fingers moved deftly over her clothes as he spoke, "I don't know how I'm going to endure not having you with me all the time during the winter, but I'll manage somehow. Your solution was . . . is . . . the only reasonable one. I've always realized that, I just couldn't cope with the idea that you could suggest it so matter-of-factly. I felt as if I were taking second place . . ."

"I understand that," Vicki interrupted softly. "I was going to explain that I only needed to be here until the end of January, and then I'd move to Manhattan, but your assumption that I must automatically subjugate my work to your lifestyle pressed every panic button I possess."

"Do you mean that? Just until the end of January?" Max tossed her last article of clothing to the floor, and began slowly, languidly, to caress her body.

"Yes, only you didn't give me the opportunity to say it." Vicki was finding it difficult to think clearly now as her senses took over under her husband's knowing hands.

"Then I'll risk January and we'll move in when you're

ready," Max murmured. "That seems the most satisfactory compromise all around. Don't you agree?"

But Vicki was incapable of answer, beyond coherent thought now as her body luxuriated in the glorious sensations that it had been missing for an eternity, it seemed.

"You are so delectable, my own wife." Max raised his head very slowly as she quivered from the peak of perfection under his mouth into breathless stillness.

"Come to me," she whispered urgently. "I must have you, my darling—a part of me, now!"

"Now and for always," Max promised, placing himself over her, at long last joining with her as she fitted her body to the familiar, well-loved contours of his with a sigh of utter contentment. Then they were spinning on the cloud that they had always shared into the glory of a togetherness founded on love, shot with the sparks of their differences, but—ultimately and forever—their *own* place.

Center Point Publishing
600 Brooks Road ● PO Box 1
Thorndike ME 04986-0001 USA

(207) 568-3717

US & Canada:
1 800 929-9108